If Wishes Were Horses

An Irish Romance

CAITLYN LYNCH

ISBN: 0-6481743-3-6

ISBN-13: 978-0-6481743-3-2

For information on my other books and forthcoming works, visit my website at caitlynlynch.com

Contents

CHAPTER ONE

"I'm sorry, could you repeat that?" Brianna pushed a finger into her other ear and moved away from the chattering crowd of her friends. "I'm afraid it's a bit noisy here." That was an understatement; she was out with her work colleagues celebrating winning a contract to create an ad campaign for a big-box appliance retailer. Beating out the bigger firms who'd been in the running was cause for serious celebration.

"Am I speaking to Miss Brianna Lane?" The voice on the other end of the phone was strongly accented, Irish, she was pretty sure.

"This is she. And you?"

"My name's Conor Morrison, Miss Lane. I'm

a solicitor in Ballina."

"Ballina, New South Wales?" Brianna couldn't think of anyone she even knew in that state. She'd been born and bred in Melbourne, had only even visited Sydney once or twice, never mind travelled to a small tourist town in the north of New South Wales.

"No, Miss Lane, Ballina in County Mayo, in the west of Ireland. I represent - *represented* - Alastair Leary."

There was a silence at the other end of the line, as though this Conor Morrison expected Brianna to know who he was talking about. Puzzled by the conversation, she made her way out of the bar entirely so she could hear properly, standing in the quiet laneway.

"I'm sorry, Mr Morrison, but I'm still in the dark as to why you're calling me."

The man at the other end emitted a quiet sigh before saying "I apologize for this, Miss Lane, but I need you to confirm your identity for me. Please would you inform me of your mother's full name, including her maiden name?"

"Sally Anne Lane, and her maiden name was Watson. Now what's this about?"

"And *her* mother's name?" the solicitor pressed.

"I never knew my grandmother, she died before I was born. Her name was Sinead Watson, but I'm afraid I don't think I ever knew her maiden name, I'm sorry." Utterly puzzled, Brianna wondered if she'd said enough.

"That's quite all right, Miss Lane. You've told me enough. You see, I was asked by Mr Leary some years ago to investigate if his sister Sinead had any living descendants. I traced you and your mother and asked Mr Leary if he wished me to make contact with you, but he declined at the time. However, he recently passed away and when the will was read, you were named as a beneficiary."

"Wait, what? Are you saying he's my… what, great-uncle?"

"That's correct, but he has, as I said, recently passed away."

"And I'm named in the will? What about Mum?" Brianna couldn't believe it. Her mother had never mentioned having any family still in Ireland; did she even know? All Brianna knew about her grandmother Sinead was that she had immigrated to Australia with her English husband back in the nineteen-sixties, Sinead herself was Irish, and she'd tragically died in a car crash when Brianna's mother was only nine.

"Your mother isn't named in the will." The

solicitor gave a polite little cough. "Do you have a legal representative I can have a copy of the paperwork couriered to?"

"I… no. I've never needed a lawyer. Dad's a barrister, though, would that be all right?"

"Certainly. I have his address here."

Of course, if he'd already investigated her and Mum, he'd have those details. Bemused, Brianna shook her head. "What did my uncle leave me? Did he have any children of his own?"

"No. For all intents and purposes, you are the last descendant of the Leary line, Miss Lane, and your great-uncle left you fifty percent of his estate."

The word *estate*, and the gravity with which the statement was delivered, made Brianna frown. "And… that consists of what?"

"I'm afraid I'm not at liberty to discuss that over the phone, Miss Lane. I'll have the papers delivered to your father's business address tomorrow; they're currently being held with an associate in Melbourne. I wish you a good evening."

The line went dead, leaving Brianna staring at her phone wondering if she'd imagined the conversation. Inheriting half the estate of a great-uncle she'd never even known existed wasn't something that happened every day.

Finally, she shrugged and headed back into the bar, greeted with catcalls from her friends for taking off and insistence the next round was on her. Laughing, she fished out her credit card and slapped it down on the bar.

Mysterious Irish inheritances would have to wait. Tonight, she was celebrating.

*   *   *

Happily, the boss had given them all the next day off, recognizing they'd all be hung over. Brianna was able to sleep in with a clear conscience.

The ringing of her phone at nine-thirty had her glaring at it with a baleful eye, but she reached out to snag it from the bedside table. A glance at the display and the strange conversation from the previous night came rushing back.

"Morning, Dad." Her voice came out a bit croaky as she pushed herself upright in bed, and she grimaced, reaching out to grab the glass of water she'd thought to pour herself before toppling into bed.

"Brianna, I've just had the strangest package of documents delivered," her father said.

"From a solicitor in Ireland?"

"That's right! Did you know about this?"

"I got a phone call last night. Apparently Grandma Watson had a brother back in Ireland. Did Mum know about him?"

"I just spoke to her, and she said she'd no idea. Your grandfather didn't talk about your grandmother much."

"He didn't talk about *anything* much." Brianna remembered her grandfather, who'd died of a heart attack when she was seventeen, as a silent sort of man. He'd been kind enough, always remembering her birthday and being very generous with his gifts, even making the effort to come to school plays and dance recitals and applaud her performances, but eight years after his death she honestly couldn't remember a single conversation they'd ever had where he'd spoken more than a dozen words.

"True," her father said, "quite true. These papers look legitimate, Bri, but I'm going to have them checked out anyway, of course."

"Is Mum annoyed? I mean, she's this guy's niece, why has he passed over her for me?" Brianna questioned.

"Goodness me, no. Your mother's delighted for you! You'll be set up for life, darling!"

Brianna reached up to rub the bridge of her nose, wishing the headache would settle down. She really shouldn't have drunk so much last night. "Dad… what did my great-uncle leave me?"

"Didn't the solicitor tell you? Alastair Leary was a rich man, Bri. He left you a half-share in his company, Leary Estates, and the other half-owner has already made an incredibly generous offer to buy you out!"

"Dad, slow down," she begged. "What's Leary Estates?"

"Oh… it's a racehorse stud. Very famous too, they've bred winners for all the big races, including a Melbourne Cup winner a few years ago. The Irish love their horses, you know." Her father chuckled. "Must be where you got it from. Your mother and I always wondered."

Brianna had to smile. She'd been pony-mad as a young girl, and even though a pony would have been impossible in their handsome urban home in a ritzy inner-Melbourne suburb, it had still been the top item on every Christmas list she'd ever written. "Must be. Racehorses, huh."

"Yes, and this offer is very generous, though of course we'll have to have the estate valued, make sure the buyer isn't trying to fleece you."

"How much?"

"Well, he's offered eight million Euros, that's the currency Ireland uses, of course, but at current exchange rates, even after you pay taxes on it, you'd get about eight million dollars."

Brianna fell out of bed with shock, dropping her phone. Scrabbling to pick it up and get it back to her ear, she choked out "I'm sorry, did you say *eight million dollars*?"

"I did, and no, I'm not having you on. There's big money in racehorses, sweetie. As I said, this will set you up for life. I'm due in court in half an hour, but I'm going to put one of my legal aides on it, get everything checked out. Why don't you come over for dinner tonight and we can talk about it?"

"Sure," she said, still in shock. "See you then."

Once her father had hung up, Brianna sat staring into space for several minutes, trying to process the sharp left turn her life had suddenly taken. While her family had always been quite comfortably off, they'd never been among the elite. She'd gone to a regular school, albeit a good one because they lived in a nice suburb, graduated college with only a small student debt thanks to her parents' help with tuition and being able to live at home throughout. Three years after graduating with a degree in Graphic Arts, she had a decent, if low-level, job designing graphics for a small ad agency, a paid-off student debt and was saving for a deposit on an apartment while sharing a rental house with three girls about her own age.

Eight million dollars. Even a tenth of that amount would set her up for life; she couldn't conceive of being so wealthy.

At last, shaking her head, she pushed herself off the floor. She needed a shower, and then she was going to take advantage of her day off. She'd take her laptop down to the coffee shop on the corner and mooch off their free wi-fi to research Leary Estates. If she was going to inherit half a racehorse stud, she really should know something about it!

CHAPTER TWO

"Hello, darling," Brianna's mother wafted a kiss against her cheek, stood back and eyed her critically. "You look nice."

Brianna gritted her teeth and told herself not to take offense to the surprised tone. "Thanks, Mum," she said instead, and sniffed the air. "Dinner smells good."

"Of course," her mother said, mouth turning down slightly at the corners. "Your father called to tell me the good news and said we should have a celebration dinner, so I made your favourite - roast lamb."

Brianna heaved an inward sigh as her mother led the way to the kitchen. Sally Lane had never quite warmed to her daughter after a dreadful pregnancy and a difficult birth, and somehow, despite Brianna growing up almost the living image of her mother, they'd never been able to close the gap between them.

"You're not upset? I mean, Alastair Leary was more closely related to you than to me. By rights, you should be the heir."

Sally turned back to look at her as they reached the kitchen, smiled without showing her teeth. "Not at all, dear. Honestly, I have a perfectly marvellous life. Your father earns good money, we own this house outright, go on lovely holidays at least twice a year, and I get all the nice clothes and things I want."

Brianna still had the feeling her mother was lying through her teeth, but putting a brave face on it since there probably wasn't a lot she could do about it anyway. Since she'd had no expectation of any inheritance, she had no grounds to contest the disposition of Great-Uncle Alastair's will - and Brianna was pretty sure her father would put paid to any such idea before it even took hold anyway.

"Well, if it really is true and I'm about to become a millionaire, I think we should all have a fabulous holiday," she said. "You always said you'd like to go to New York one day. You and I could hit the boutiques and Dad could go check out some of those fancy golf courses he's always drooling over in his golf magazines."

Her suggestion earned a true smile from Sally. "That's a lovely idea, Bri. Perhaps we'll do just that." She opened the fridge and pulled out a bottle of champagne. "To New York, hm?"

"Absolutely!" Brianna agreed, going to fetch glasses from the dresser. She was pouring a glass for each of them when the sound of the front door closing told them her father had arrived. A minute or two later he joined them in the kitchen, smiling warmly and coming to kiss her mother's cheek and hug her warmly.

"My little girl, a millionaire," he said with a chuckle.

"Dad." She shook her head, laughing at him and kissing his whiskered cheek. "Did your legal assistant find out any more? I looked up Leary Estates, their website looked impressive."

She'd been quite stunned, actually. The estate appeared to have two parts, the stallion residence and the breeding farm where the mares and foals stayed. The stallion farm had twelve stallions at stud and every one of them had won multiple races in their own right and gone on to sire more successful racers. A little bit of clicking, and she'd discovered the fee to send a mare to even the cheapest of the stallions for breeding was absolutely eye-watering.

"It's all for real, sweetie." Her father accepted the glass of wine Sally offered him, and took a seat at the kitchen table.

"I went through some papers and found my mother's birth certificate," Sally said unexpectedly. "She was born Sinead Leary in a place called Ballina."

"That's where the solicitor said he was from," Brianna said, watching as her mother took a small stack of papers from the kitchen counter and put them down in front of her father. "What do you remember about her, Mum? I can't remember you ever talking about her, really."

"Darling, she died when I was a child," Sally shook her head regretfully. "I barely remember her, and Dad never talked about her. I dug out a box of his things and found these; some letters they exchanged, her birth certificate and their marriage certificate - they married in London. She was working there as a nurse, or so the letters say."

"Why did they emigrate?" Brianna pressed.

"Father was offered a job. He was a surgeon, you know." Sally had always been very proud of her father. "He was offered a position with the cardiology department at the Royal Melbourne Hospital and decided to take it."

"And Grandmother never wanted to go back to Ireland?"

Sally shrugged helplessly. "I've no idea, darling. I only have a couple of photos of her, even." She handed Brianna an old photo album. "There are wedding photos on the first couple of pages, and one photo of her with me as a baby."

It was like looking into a faded mirror. Sinead Watson, née Leary, looked exactly like her daughter Sally... and everyone had been telling Brianna since her early teens she was the image of her mother. Sinead shared their nut-brown hair, creamy complexions and dark green eyes, her nose tip-tilted just like Brianna and Sally's.

"Wow," Brianna murmured, studying the photograph of the pretty young woman in the white lacy wedding gown, the photograph faded so the dress looked more yellow than white. "That's... a little bit freaky, actually."

"I hadn't looked at them for years, either," Sally admitted. "But I went through everything, and there's nothing about her life before she was nursing in London, apart from her birth certificate. Nothing at all."

"In those days, a young woman leaving country Ireland to go and work in London was quite possibly a little scandalous," Brianna's father remarked, looking up from the papers. "I wonder if her family disowned her."

"I daresay we'll never know now, with her brother gone," Sally said.

Brianna bit her lip, staring at the smiling young woman, the bride from sixty years ago. *What were your secrets?* she wondered silently as her mother bustled about, pulling the roast leg of lamb from the oven. *Why did you leave home, Sinead? What drove you from a comfortable life among the horse farms and green fields of Ireland?*

"We should find a business appraiser," her father said, looking up from the papers in front of him. "In Dublin, I suppose, though we might need to have one fly in from London. Find out if this…" he sifted the papers in front of him briefly, found what he was looking for. "This Declan O'Siorain's offer is a fair one." He stumbled over the unfamiliar Irish name, pronounced it 'O'Show-rain'.

"I want to go see it."

Brianna wasn't even sure where the words had come from, when the idea had popped into her head. Perhaps it was that morning at the coffee shop, when she'd found herself sighing wistfully over the photographs she'd found on the Leary Estates website, the rolling green hills, the mares and foals grazing on lush grass beside a shimmering blue lake.

"What?" Her mother screeched it, startled. "You? Go to Ireland? Of course not!"

Her father took his glasses off, laid them down on the table and gave her a considering look. "Let Bri speak, Sally. She's not a child any more. Sit down, Bri, and talk to me. Have you thought this through? Can you get holiday leave from your job? Because think about it… you're only twenty-five. Even eight million dollars isn't enough for you to quit working and live a life of luxury."

"I know that." She chewed on her lip, thinking. "I can still work even if I'm not in the office, though."

"Even with this new contract?" Her father's eyes were knowing. "You were all excited when you called me about it yesterday. Is that all forgotten now there might be some money coming your way?"

"No!" She scowled at him. "You raised me better than that - both of you. I have responsibilities, and I'm not running away from them. I can work remotely, my laptop has all the software I need. All I need is a wi-fi connection and I can find that even in the more remote parts of Ireland, I'm sure. But," leaning forward, she beseeched her father to understand, "this inheritance is a responsibility too.

This… Declan O'Siorain, he's inherited the other half, right? So if my great-uncle wanted him to have the whole estate, he could either have left it all to him, or sold out to him before he died and then left me some money, right?"

Andrew Lane considered his daughter thoughtfully for a few moments before nodding slowly.

"You can't seriously be considering letting her go!" Sally cried.

"Sally," he turned his attention to his wife, "how am I supposed to stop her? Bri's an adult, and she can make her own decisions. Unless you're asking us for a loan to pay for your flights?"

For a moment she considered it, but no. "I've got savings."

"That's for your deposit on a house!" Sally was obviously still very much against the idea.

"Those documents are legitimate, Sal. I'd stake my reputation on it. A few thousand in savings is small potatoes compared to her inheritance. If you want to go over there and take a look, why not?" Andrew shrugged. "Maybe even go anonymously. Meet with the business appraiser and get them to take you in as an 'assistant'." His grin was mischievous. "It'll be interesting to see the underside of the business, rather than have the red carpet rolled out for you as the new half-owner, won't it?"

Brianna's eyes sparkled as she grinned back at him. "I love the way you think, Dad."

"You've got a brain, Bri. I trust you to use it. And we're always here if you need advice, or someone to talk to. Both of us." Andrew shot a warning look at Sally, who sighed and crossed the kitchen to put a hand on Brianna's shoulder.

"Of course we are, darling. I just worry... it's so far away."

"The world's a smaller place these days, Mum." Brianna reached up to cover her mother's fingers with her own. "We'll Skype, and you can see for yourself I'm fine."

CHAPTER THREE

"Yes, Mum, I'm *fine*." Brianna resisted the urge to roll her eyes. "I've been in Ireland three hours; all I've seen so far is the taxi ride from the airport to the hotel."

"You promised you'd call *as soon* as you got in," her mother scolded. Even on the small screen of her phone, Brianna could see Sally's brows were pinched together with worry.

"Forgive me. I was starving; I felt a bit queasy on the plane, couldn't eat. I took the time to have a decent breakfast so you could hear me talk instead of listening to my stomach growling."

Sally's expression lightened a little at the joke. "Are you jet lagged?"

"Probably, though right now I feel wide

awake." She'd slept a lot more than she expected to on the long flight to Knock in the west of Ireland, via Bangkok and London. Though she'd paid for her own ticket, her father had quietly used some saved-up frequent flyer points to upgrade her to business class and she'd had a lay-flat bed on the long flights.

"When are you meeting the business valuer?"

"He's driving from Dublin today and will meet me this evening. I'll let you know how it all goes, I promise."

It took several minutes to finally disengage, but Brianna managed it at last and turned off the app with a sigh of relief before jumping to her feet. Wide awake and full of a hearty breakfast, she was eager to get out and explore.

She'd originally thought she would stay in Ballina, where the solicitor who'd contacted her was based, but a little research and a conversation with the business broker they'd found in Dublin convinced her it would be better to stay closer to the stud farm. The broker was amenable to the deception of having her pose as an assistant as long as she covered costs, so she'd found a country house hotel less than a mile from the main property of Leary Estates and asked the broker to book two rooms for the week under the business name. The receptionist hadn't so much as blinked an eye when she checked in, hadn't even asked for ID.

Gazing out of her hotel window at the view, Brianna hugged herself with delight. The hotel stood on a small promontory overlooking at a small distance a lake, Lough Conn, blue water glinting under the summer sunshine. Having come from the grey dreariness of a cold, rainy winter in Melbourne, the sunshine made her eager to go out.

Ten minutes later, she was walking away from the hotel with a map the helpful receptionist had given her stuffed in her jeans pocket. While the road didn't follow the lough here on the western shore, there was a walking trail through the woods which led down to it... and, helpfully for Brianna's purposes, actually passed alongside the border of the Leary Estate for part of the way.

The property maps she'd obtained showed this part of the estate was partially located on a peninsula jutting out into the lake. The main house itself was on the lakeshore, the stables located a little closer to the road, and there was a couple hundred acres of grazing paddocks surrounding it all.

A few minutes' walk through the woods brought her the lake into view ahead of her, and to her right the trees gave way to grassy fields with heavy post-and-rail fencing painted a bright white. At her first sight of the property which was now half hers, Brianna couldn't resist stopping and leaning on the fence to gaze at the view.

There were horses in the field before her, a dapple grey mare grazing peacefully and a foal with a darker coat, gleaming almost black in the sunshine, gambolling in the grass - chasing butterflies, Brianna realized, smiling at the foal's antics. *What a cutie*.

She could see half a dozen similarly fenced fields, each occupied by a single mare with a foal. She wondered why the horses weren't kept together so the foals couldn't play with each other, and then shook her head as the reason dawned on her. These weren't just any foals; each one could be worth a small, or even a large, fortune. Letting them play together invited injury which could render a valuable animal completely worthless.

Following the path, and the fence line, brought Brianna down to the lakeshore. The fence turned away to the right and followed the shore, but there was a large *Private Property; No Trespassing* sign erected at the corner of the fence making it quite clear that part of the lakeshore was private. She could see the house from her current vantage point, a large whitewashed building with a grey tiled roof, and part of what she thought must be the stable roof a little further away.

After gazing her fill, Brianna finally sighed and turned to make her way back to the hotel. She'd learn nothing looking at the estate from outside the boundary, but getting an inside look would have to wait until tomorrow.

*   *   *

"Charlie, don't turn Lansdowne Lass out today," Declan instructed. "She's very restless, I think she'll drop today or tonight."

"Got it, sorr," Charlie touched his cap, and Declan scowled at him.

"Will you quit that?"

"You're the boss now, Dec. Gotta show respect in front of the lads." The grizzled old stable manager, who'd known Declan since he was just a boy hanging over the fence gazing wistfully at the horses out in the fields, grinned at him.

"Give over. Why don't you retire? The old man made you rich in the will. Leave these boys to me."

Charlie only laughed. "Eh, I'm not worried about the lads. It's the horses would run roughshod over you if I left you to it."

Declan laughed back, shaking his head.

"You're the softest touch of all. I saw you with molasses on your fingers this morning, bribing Miss Menace into behaving for you."

Charlie's expression of innocence wouldn't have fooled even the most naive. Declan clapped his friend's shoulder and made his way across the stable yard, critical eye noting a few wisps of straw drifting in the breeze. Catching the eye of one of the younger stable hands, he gestured the boy over and pointed out the issue.

"That business broker will be here shortly. I want the place immaculate."

"Wouldn't it be better for it to be a bit messy, sorr? Make him think it's worth less than it really is?"

"Leave the thinking to me, Padraic. Get your broom out." Declan watched as the teenager hurried to do his bidding. Looking about, he thought everything was in order; maybe he should hop in his car and drive over to Ballybronn, the other property where the stallion yard was. No, they weren't due to visit Ballybronn with the broker until the afternoon, and Charlie was going over there once morning rounds were finished here. Charlie would see to it everything was all in readiness.

He didn't have time, anyway. A quick glance at his watch and he muttered a curse under his breath, turning to head back to the house with long, swift strides. He needed to wash up and change before the city folks arrived; he didn't want to look like some hayseed yokel with horse shit on his jeans and a ragged old flannel shirt one of the foals had ripped when tugging on it playfully as he turned the little swine out with his mother.

The broker was right on time; the sound of a car on the driveway made him hurry back down the stairs without bothering to comb his hair; a shove of his fingers through it would have to do. Fionn in the office must have buzzed them in at the gate, since nobody could just drive in and no-one else was expected today.

Declan exited the house in time to watch with a jaundiced eye as a gleaming black Range Rover drew up in front, a man and a woman getting out. This must be the business broker, Liam Connolly, and the assistant Connolly said he'd be bringing along to take notes.

Connolly was the epitome of a city slicker in his designer suit and shiny shoes, Declan thought with carefully hidden disgust as he moved forward to introduce himself and shake the man's hand. At least the assistant had dressed sensibly, blue jeans and sturdy shoes, a form-fitting black T-shirt drawing Declan's eyes to her shapely figure before

33

he looked away, hastily kicking himself.

Connolly didn't seem to think much of his assistant since he didn't even bother introducing her. Declan wasn't about to be that rude to a lady, though, so he deliberately offered his hand and said his name. Wide green eyes flew to his face briefly before the girl dropped them shyly and took his hand.

"I'm Bri," she mumbled.

There was something familiar about her, but Declan couldn't quite put his finger on what. Inviting them into the house, he studied her surreptitiously, noting the way she looked avidly around, taking everything in. She was a pretty thing, he conceded to himself, thick dark brown hair caught back in a ponytail, creamy soft skin with a few freckles sprinkled across the bridge of her tip-tilted nose. Probably in her mid-twenties, she was young enough to be Connolly's daughter, not that Declan thought she was. The pair looked nothing alike, and he was ignoring her besides.

CHAPTER FOUR

Brianna's skin prickled, and she just *knew* Declan was watching her again. Did he know who she was? Of course, if her great-uncle had her investigated, he might have photographs, and he might have shown them to Declan... he might be waiting for her to reveal herself.

Sneaking a glance at him, she discovered he was actually not looking at her at all, had his eyes firmly on the heavily pregnant mare whose stall they stood outside. Blushing, she chewed on the end of her pen. It was a good thing Mr Connolly had told her he didn't really need her to take notes; he was recording everything on his phone for later review.

She peeked at Declan again under her lashes. Why hadn't she thought to research him as well as the estate? He was a lot younger than she'd expected, not much more than thirty, she guessed, and seriously good-looking, around six feet tall with broad shoulders and strong arms, thick muscles swelling from the sleeves of his short-sleeved T-shirt. His dark brown hair was a little long, curling in an unruly way at the back of his neck and over his ears, his skin tan from hours spent out in all weathers, slight crinkles at the corners of dark blue eyes.

Those eyes slid over towards her again then, and she snatched her gaze away. *Stop staring!* she ordered herself. *You're going to make him suspicious!*

Brianna tried to focus on her surroundings instead. The house, which Declan had said was called Galamor, was even more beautiful inside than out, with antique timber furniture polished to a glossy shine and thickly upholstered, comfortable chairs. Mr Connolly was eyeing the paintings on the wall with a connoisseur's eye, asking Declan questions about the artists and the provenance of the paintings.

A pretty middle-aged Irish woman brought in a

tray with tea and some shortbread biscuits, and Brianna sat sipping her tea, nibbling on a biscuit and taking in everything around her. The house and its contents alone were magnificent, like a stately home.

"How old is the house?" she asked quietly during a break in the conversation.

"There's been a house on the site since the fourteenth century, though Galamor as it stands now was finished in 1745." Declan gave her a curious stare. "You're not Irish?"

"She's here on a transfer program. Just an intern." Mr Connolly cut him off quickly, shot Brianna a warning glance. She was already kicking herself; knowing her accent would give her away as Australian, she'd resolved to say as little as possible. Pressing her lips firmly together, she vowed not to say another word.

Declan gave them a quick tour of the inside of the house. The bedrooms were as beautifully furnished as the reception rooms, all seven of them, and Brianna was surprised to see every one of them had a modern ensuite bathroom attached. She whispered a quick question to Connolly, who asked Declan when the bathrooms were installed.

"About ten years ago. Mr Leary spent two months in America buying new bloodstock for the stud, and decided to take the opportunity to modernize the house. The kitchen was refitted at the same time, discreet solar panels put on the roof, rainwater tanks attached to the stables." Declan smiled at their impressed looks. "The house actually had eleven bedrooms and only three bathrooms before. Occasionally an owner would come to stay for a few days, and Mr Leary thought it would be better to have more modern conveniences."

"I daresay it's increased the value of the house quite significantly," Mr Connolly said with a nod, and they moved on, taking a different set of stairs to the ones they'd ascended back down to the ground floor.

"Those were the servants' stairs, originally," Declan said, "and this is the service wing of the house… the kitchen, pantry, laundry, boot room."

Since he had said the kitchen had been updated, Brianna had half expected a restaurant-style modern kitchen with stainless steel and glass everywhere, but that wasn't at all what they found when Declan pushed open a door. Instead, there was a huge red enamel stove and a scrubbed pine table, cabinets of a light stained wood topped with honey-coloured marble, and even a large squashy couch beneath the large windows at the far side of the room. A tabby cat asleep on the couch raised its head to give them a sleepy green stare, and the woman who'd brought in their tea stood up from her seat at the table where she'd been shelling peas into a bowl.

It was the most beautiful, most homely room Brianna had ever seen. She wanted to plop herself down on the couch and pet the tabby cat, soak in the room's warm and friendly glow.

Mr Connolly had to grab her elbow and almost pull her out of the room as they moved on, and Brianna couldn't stop wistfully looking back over her shoulder as they exited the house by a rear door.

"You'll need to get an art appraiser in," the broker murmured quietly in her ear as they followed Declan past a large kitchen garden toward the stable block. "I think one of those paintings was a Gainsborough. The art collection might be worth more than everything else put together."

"Is it part of the estate?"

"I believe so. We can check the paperwork back at the hotel."

"Do you know someone?" Brianna hoped he did, then she wouldn't have to research and contact yet another expert herself.

"I do, actually; he's from the auctioneer Sotheby's in Dublin. I've consulted him before when a business I was appraising had significant art assets. I'll call him when we finish here today."

"Thanks."

Declan had stopped before opening a gate, was waiting for them. Connolly gave him a polite smile. "Just giving my assistant some notes to take down."

At least she'd thought to bring a notebook, Brianna thought, fishing it hastily out of her bag and finding a pen as Declan looked at her curiously. She scribbled *art appraiser Sotheby's Gainsborough???* on the first page and smiled tightly as he kept looking at her. Finally he looked away and opened the gate.

"As you're aware, Galamor is the larger of the two properties which make up the estate. The other property, Ballybronn, is the stallion yard, which has facility to hold a dozen stallions, though at the present time we only have eleven standing there. Galamor is the broodmare and foal facility, and we have stabling for seventy mares and foals here in specially built stabling, plus forty other short-term mare-only stalls for the mares who come to be put to the studs. Sixteen of the mares are fully owned by Leary Estates and are permanent residents here, and the rest transition in and out. At the present time, we are completely full up. Most of the season's crop of foals have already been born and the mares and foals spend part of the day outside in individually fenced paddocks."

"*Most* of the foals?" Connolly queried as they stopped outside one of the few occupied stables. The doors were open, a steel chain the only barrier keeping the horse inside. Though Brianna was pretty sure the mare had no intention of making a bid for freedom. She stood drowsing on a thick bed of clean straw, pregnant belly grossly distended.

"This is Lansdowne Lass, one of our own mares," Declan said, and Brianna looked at him in surprise, because up until that moment his tone had been crisp, all business. As he spoke of the horse, though, his voice lowered and softened, and when she looked at him, she saw a gentle smile on his face. He loved the horses, she thought, truly loved them.

"She's in foal to Oracular, one of our top sires. His stud fee is seventy thousand euros a cover."

Brianna's jaw dropped. Some of the stallions at the Leary Estate had fees marked 'price on application' on the website, and they would also only agree to accept mares whose bloodlines had been vetted and approved. She'd truly had no idea of the astronomical sums involved with the very best stallions.

Apparently the business broker knew, though,

41

because he just nodded with no sign of surprise. Of course, he'd already received copies of the business's books from the last five years to examine; this inspection of the property was the final step in his evaluation process. Presumably he knew all about the stud fees, how much the estate charged for a mare to be bred to each stallion and how many such breedings occurred per year.

She was going to be asking a lot of questions at dinner that evening, Brianna thought, and with that she started using her notebook in earnest, writing down things she wanted to ask for clarification on as the two men talked.

Oddly, now she was doing the job she'd supposedly been brought along for, Declan still spent a substantial portion of his time looking at her. Brianna caught his eyes any number of times as they progressed around Galamor, touring the stable block, the storage areas, the feed mixing room, a row of little cabins where the stable hands who lived in stayed.

"They get three meals a day as part of their compensation package," Declan said. "Molly, who you met up at the house, keeps house and feeds all our hungry mouths. Her husband is our vet."

"You employ your own full-time vet?" Mr Connolly asked with a frown.

"Yes. We need him here every day, believe me. Every mare has to have blood tests and a health exam before they go to the stallions, and we can have over a thousand mares a season come through. If we were paying standard consultancy rates the vet bills would be astronomical... never mind the call-out fees for difficult midnight births!" Declan smiled, the corners of his eyes crinkling up again and making Brianna's knees go weak.

"He lives on site?"

"He and Molly share a cottage near the boundary between Galamor and Ballybronn. Rent free in part exchange for their labour, of course."

"That seems a common theme here," Connolly remarked. Brianna bit her tongue. It seemed a perfectly sensible arrangement to her, but Connolly sounded quite snide about it. She shot him a glare under her lashes, stopping only when she caught Declan giving her a puzzled look.

CHAPTER FIVE

There was something off about Liam Connolly's assistant, and Declan couldn't for the life of him figure out what. She was scribbling away in her notebook, but when he sneaked a quick glance over her shoulder she seemed to be writing more questions rather than taking notes on his answers. She never said a word he could hear, but he caught her whispering to Connolly a time or two, and he also caught her glaring at the broker with nothing short of fury in her expression once.

As they returned to the house for lunch before going across to Ballybronn, he couldn't take his eyes off her. She wasn't exactly hard on the eyes either, he admitted privately, though he tried to kid himself into believing that wasn't why he was looking at her. There was something not quite right, and his instincts were screaming at him to find out what.

The big kitchen was full, the stable lads and lasses taking their seats at the big pine table and helping themselves from the platters of sandwiches laid out. Connolly's nose wrinkled with distaste, but Bri took a seat between two of the youngest with a friendly smile and accepted a plate one of them passed her.

Declan would have liked to sit closer, hear what she had to say, but there were only two seats left at the far end of the table and he had to sit down by Connolly and look at the man's sneer at having to share a table and a meal with stable hands. He found himself watching Bri instead, watching her long-fingered, delicate hands as she lifted her water glass to sip, the way her lips curved up as she smiled at one of the stable-lad's clumsy jokes.

The afternoon passed much the same as the morning, though Bri seemed even more awed by the magnificent Thoroughbred stallions at Ballybronn than she had been by the mares. They arrived just as Charlie was bringing Prestigious out of his stall to go to the stallion barn and Bri's eyes went very wide and round.

"Stand clear," Declan reached out a hand to stop her as she took an unconscious step towards the magnificent stallion, prancing elegantly across the yard, ears pricked and tail held high. "He's got a nasty temper, that one."

"Isn't that an undesirable trait?" She turned those huge green eyes up to him, seeming to forget she was avoiding speaking to him until the words were actually out of her mouth.

"Normally yes, but Prestigious won seven Group One races in his racing career, and his offspring have won dozens more, bad temper included." He shrugged. "For enough money, you can put up with bad behaviour."

"Women certainly put up with badly-behaved men for enough money!" Connolly interrupted with a braying laugh. "Eh? Eh?"

Bri's look of dislike was even more intense than Declan's, and he suddenly wondered if her boss sexually harassed her. Connolly seemed like the type. Instinctively Declan moved a fraction closer to Bri, curled his fingers lightly around her elbow.

"Come and meet Oracular instead. He's, well, not exactly docile, I doubt you could call any Thoroughbred stallion docile, but he's gentle. Never tried to bite or kick any of my stable hands

47

yet."

She didn't try to pull away as he led her across the yard to the prime box, where Oracular leaned on his door and whinnied eagerly to Declan.

"Yes, you know you're the prince, don't you?" Declan murmured, running the long white stripe down the black stallion's nose.

"He's beautiful," Bri murmured. "Could I pet him?"

"Sure. Put your hand against his cheek, here, and run your fingers under his jaw. He loves a good scratch there."

Oracular extended his jaw, eyes closing with bliss as Bri scratched, and she laughed. "You big old softy. I didn't bring you any treats."

"Here." Declan always had something in his jacket pocket. He handed Bri a couple of compressed green pellets, about to tell her to hold her hand flat with the treat on her palm when she did so without prompting. "You've handled horses before?" he asked as Oracular lipped up the treats.

"I was pony mad as a kid. We lived in the city, though." She looked wistful, gave Oracular one last scratch under the jaw before stepping back. "I haven't been on a horse in, oh, must be ten years."

He wanted to ask more, get her talking about her childhood in that softly musical, accented voice, but Liam Connolly cleared his throat pointedly and asked a question.

Stop talking to a girl you're never going to see again and concentrate on what really matters. Declan made himself turn away.

"Yes, we can accommodate another stallion. Of course, most of them are owned by syndicates; only Oracular is entirely the property of the Leary Estate."

Connolly's brow furrowed. "All of Prestigious' stud fees were included in the last three years' accounts, though, as being estate revenue."

"That's correct, but Prestigious was excluded from the estate in Mr Leary's will. He was left to Charlie, Mr Leary's stable manager."

Connolly looked quite disapproving, and Bri cocked her head and gave Declan a curious look, though she said nothing. He had the impression there had been a question on the tip of her tongue and she'd bitten it back.

"That makes a significant dent in the estate's revenue stream," Connolly muttered.

"It does," Declan agreed, "but I've consulted with the bank about the loan I'll need to take out to purchase the remainder of the business from the other owner, and the bank are quite comfortable I'll be able to service the loan with the remaining revenue stream."

"*If* you only need to borrow eight million," Connolly said depressingly, and Declan's jaw clenched. Eight million was the absolute maximum the bank would lend him, but if the broker valued the business too high and the other owner insisted on putting it on the open market, he'd have no hope. There'd be a bidding war and they'd be snapped up and absorbed into one of the bigger studs, and though he'd be a millionaire in his own right he'd still lose the only thing which had ever mattered to him.

Bri was looking sideways at him under her lashes, an unreadable expression on her face. Declan made himself smile, even though he knew it probably came out more like a grimace. "Shall we move on?"

They finished touring Ballybronn and walked back along the track to Galamor. He should probably offer them tea again but honestly he just wanted them gone so he could pour himself a large shot of whisky and drown his sorrows in it. Escorting them straight to Connolly's flash Range Rover, he bade the man a polite farewell before stepping in front of Bri and opening the passenger door for her. She shot him a surprised glance, and he offered his hand.

"It was nice to meet you, Bri."

"Likewise," she said after a moment, accepting his hand with a small smile. For a mad moment he thought about asking for her phone number, asking if she ever got out of Dublin for the weekend, before shaking himself out of it. A city girl was the last thing he needed.

"Goodbye." He let go of her hand, waited until she was inside the car before closing the door for her, and watched the car disappear down the drive with a sigh of relief.

Molly glanced up from stirring a big pot on the stove as he entered the kitchen, smirked at him. "Thinking with the head atop your shoulders yet?"

"What do you mean?" He frowned at her.

"Oh come on, Dec, you had eyes for nothing but that girl all afternoon." She looked highly entertained, and he flopped into a chair at the kitchen table with a groan.

"Leave it out, Molly."

"First time I've ever seen you moon over a girl like that."

"I said leave it out!"

She laughed at him. Molly had known him since he was a baby, had no compunctions about poking a little fun. "Ah, you never had a look in anyway, Dec."

"Why do you say that?" She sounded so certain, he couldn't help but be curious.

"For sure, they've booked in for the week at Duncarrick, haven't they?"

"What?" Declan stared at her, startled. "They're not going back to Dublin tonight?" It was only four in the afternoon, and about a four-hour drive back to the city. He'd assumed they were only staying the one night, but Molly's sister Moira and her husband owned the Duncarrick Hotel. Moira was an infallible source.

"Staying a week." Molly nodded knowledgeably. "Moira asked me about it, wanted to know what on earth they'd be taking a week to do."

"They're sharing a room?" Declan felt quite unreasonably disappointed.

"Booked two rooms, haven't they, under the business name, but for sure that's a cover in case his wife calls to check on him, Moira says. They had their heads very close over dinner last night, whispering and going quiet as soon as she came near."

"I see." So all their ignoring each other had been just an act, then.

Now he *really* needed a whisky.

CHAPTER SIX

Declan came back in from the yard the following morning, brow furrowed with concern. Lansdowne Lass still hadn't gone into labour, and though Ted, his vet and Molly's husband, wasn't concerned, Declan was. The Lass was a first-time mother and looking quite distressed. He intended to grab a quick sandwich and go back out to stay with her, however long it took.

Molly's sister Moira was in the kitchen, though, helping dish up lunch, and Declan had too much time to brood in the last few hours.

"Thought you'd be with your guests at the hotel, Moira," he remarked. "Or have they not come out of their room?"

"Arah, I was just talkin' to Molly about that,"

Moira said with a grin. "I think I might have got the wrong end of the stick after all, because Mr Connolly headed back to Dublin this morning, cheerful as you please."

Declan blinked. "They didn't stay?"

"*He* didn't stay. The lass is still with us. Says she's staying the week at least."

That made no sense. Declan stared at Moira, and then at Molly, who shrugged to show her own incomprehension.

"Why would he leave an intern here for a week on her own? Does she even have her own car?"

"No," Moira shook her head. "Came in yesterday morning by taxi from Knock, she did. Lovely girl, she's been telling me all about Melbourne…"

"Melbourne, *Australia*?"

"Well yes, of course." Moira gave him a strange look. "Did you not speak to her? Plain as day, that accent, I picked it out at once. Been watching *Neighbours* too much, haven't I," she nudged Molly and laughed.

"Bri," Declan said to Molly, who'd clearly put two and two together as well and looked as shocked as he felt. "*Brianna* Lane."

"Is she famous or something?" Moira asked eagerly.

"She's the other heir," Molly said when Declan couldn't speak. A red mist of rage was rising up in front of his eyes.

The sneaky, lying little bitch. Coming here under false pretences, looking everything over with avaricious eyes, no doubt whispering in Connolly's ear to make sure the broker didn't miss a single thing that might have value, so she could squeeze every last dollar out of the place. If he got his hands on her, he'd…

He'd…

The memory of those huge green eyes swam across his mind, and he shook it off furiously. She'd played him, portrayed herself as innocent and shy, and now he was totally sure that was a lie too. He'd never in his life struck a woman, he'd never so much as smacked one of his mares, but if Bri had been in front of him right then he'd be very tempted to put his hands around her neck.

"Dec," Molly's soft voice brought him out of the red rage; she was looking at him anxiously. "Don't go doing anything foolish, now."

The muscles along his jaw clenched. "I'm not contemplating murder, Molly. Not seriously, anyway. That wouldn't solve my problem anyway, would it?" He'd only end up with whoever was Brianna's heir. Probably her parents; he knew from

Alastair's file she was an only child.

"What are you going to do?" Moira asked in a small voice. "Do you want me to speak to her, ask what's she's planning?"

"No." Rubbing a hand over his brow, Declan sighed. "No. I need some time to think. Don't say anything to her, Moira."

"Maybe she needs time to think too," Moira pointed out sensibly. "She's only a young lass, after all. Reckon this has all come as quite a shock to her, too. At least you knew Alastair was splitting the estate; I don't think she ever even knew he existed."

"Did she tell you that?" Declan frowned; that seemed naive of Brianna. This was the country, where everybody knew everyone else. Talking about a big inheritance was bound to be gossip-worthy.

"No, but she did say something about this being the last place she'd expected to be. I'm just adding two and two together now I know who she is." Moira shrugged. "You were the one who said Alastair told his man not to make contact."

"I don't think he'd decided at that point," Declan said quietly. "I think he wanted to know who his sister's descendants were, if they were worthy, before he made up his mind." And Alastair *had* decided Brianna was worthy; Alastair who

Declan had loved like a father, had respected more than any other person he'd ever known.

Heaving a deep sigh, he grabbed one of the sandwiches from the platter Molly had just finished preparing. "I'm going back to Lansdowne Lass. I'll be in her stall if anyone's looking for me. Don't spread it around who Brianna is, please. I don't want her to know *we* know."

He waited for their nods of acknowledgment before heading back out the door, stuffing the sandwich into his mouth as he went.

Lansdowne Lass was standing spraddle-legged in the straw when he got back, her noble head held low.

"Hey, Lass." Declan stroked one drooping ear gently, and she huffed, rolling a great dark eye at him. "You don't look like you're having a good day either."

She couldn't answer him, of course. Gently, he reached to stroke her belly, feeling around. The foal wasn't moving around at the moment, not that there was much room in there.

Finally Declan moved back, going to sit on a spare straw bale he'd brought in. Leaning back against the wall he closed his eyes and tried to think, tried to recall everything Bri had said the previous day. All he could seem to remember was her expression of innocent delight as she patted Oracular's regal head, though, and with a growl he opened his eyes again. She *wasn't* innocent, she'd been there under false pretences, and her pretty face and sweet smile sure as hell wouldn't fool him a second time!

He'd spent the previous night in a sleeping bag in the straw in a corner of the Lass's stable, so he hadn't had much sleep. Drowsing off leaning on the wall, he startled awake when the mare let out a low groan.

"Hey, Lass." Pushing himself up off the bale with a grunt of his own as his stiff back protested, he went to the mare, now lying down on her side and panting heavily. He could already see it, though, the skin over her belly rippling as the contraction pulsed through her. "All right, sweet girl. Looks like your baby's ready to come." He kept his voice low and soothing, stroking the Lass's neck and shoulder as she quivered and groaned again.

Fishing his phone from his pocket, Declan sent a quick text to Ted and then another to Charlie. The vet would be over at the stallion barn supervising, but he'd get there as soon as he could. Declan had probably attended as many foalings as the vet by now anyway; there wasn't much he couldn't handle unless the mare started a profuse bleed or things went seriously wrong and she needed a Caesarean section. The stable was one of their special 'birthing pens' which was all set up to perform the surgery if they had to, but Declan really hoped it wouldn't be necessary.

"Easy, Lass, easy." Another contraction rippled across her belly and suddenly there was a great gush of fluid at her hindquarters, quickly absorbed into the thick straw on the stable floor.

"Here we go." He'd wrapped her tail earlier to help keep it out of the way, moved around to crouch down behind her now and check. No sign yet of the foal's nose, but it wouldn't be long; equine births were fast.

He had his back to the stable door, so when he heard the sound of footsteps scraping on the concrete outside, he assumed it was either Charlie or Ted arriving.

"Get in here," Declan said crisply, "this is happening, right now."

"The foal's coming?"

He whipped around, stared at Brianna standing in the doorway. "*You.*"

She took a small step back under his ferocious glare. "Hi. Molly said you were here…"

He narrowed his eyes at her.

"She told me you know."

"Why are you here?" he asked bluntly.

CHAPTER SEVEN

Brianna quailed under Declan's glare, but she wasn't about to flee. "I'm here to apologize," she said in response to his question.

If anything, his glower darkened. "Moira told you we figured you out, then?" he said gruffly.

"No. I walked to the house and knocked on the door. Molly's expression of disappointment told me you'd already guessed what I'd come to confess."

Lansdowne Lass groaned, a low, terrible sound, and Brianna moved forward instinctively. "Please let me help. I could hold her head, comfort her…"

Declan's jaw worked, and she could almost see the moment he realized he couldn't just order her off the property. "Fine," he said curtly. "But only until Charlie or Ted arrive. I need experienced hands here."

She couldn't blame him for the sentiment. Letting herself into the stall, she knelt beside the mare's head, reached to lightly stroke the sweat-dampened neck. "Easy, girl. Everything's gonna be all right," she crooned, doing her best to keep her voice low and gentle, reassuring to the distressed animal.

Declan grunted, and Brianna looked across the mare's body at him. "Everything okay?"

"Front hooves and nose are out," he said tersely. "Won't be long now."

"That was quick!"

"Equine labour usually is. If it lasts more than an hour, something's seriously wrong. Come on now, Lass, you can do it," Declan exhorted, patting the Lass's rump gently. "Come on now, push that head out."

The mare groaned again and Brianna watched with fascination, seeing the hide over her belly ripple with another contraction. Declan gave a cry of triumph.

"That's it, darlin'!"

Brianna craned her neck to see, watching as Declan moved back, pulling carefully on two tiny hooves, and suddenly the foal slid completely free onto the straw.

"Oh, my God," Brianna breathed in amazement, watching as Declan used a handful of clean straw to wipe the majority of the mess from the foal's body before carefully lifting him and bringing him to the mare's head. Lass was already looking for her baby, her head lifting and swinging around, soft little nickers emitting from her nostrils until the foal was laid right beside her. At once she began to wash him clean and Brianna smiled with joy.

"You're gonna be a wonderful mama," she whispered, moving back herself to give the new mother time and space to bond with her baby. Looking up at Declan she saw again the fondly loving smile on his face as he gazed down at the miracle of new life.

The smile faded as Declan met her eyes.

"Damn, we missed it!" a voice exclaimed, making them both look away.

"Out," Declan said, jerking his head towards the door where two men stood watching them. "We'll let Ted finish up here. You and I need to talk."

Ted was the vet, Brianna remembered, Molly's husband. A smallish man with salt-and-pepper hair and a lot of laugh lines around his eyes, he looked curiously at her as Declan held the stable door open for her to exit. The other man with him, Charlie, she recognized from her earlier tour. He was the stable manager her great-uncle had left the valuable stallion Prestigious to. He obviously hadn't heard about her identity yet, because he gave her a befuddled look and said "Declan, what…" before a sharp wave of Declan's hand cut him off.

"Later," Declan said. "This way, Miss *Lane*."

Charlie's wide eyes told her he'd put two and two together, and Brianna heaved an inward sigh as she followed Declan. Maybe coming here undercover hadn't been such a bright idea after all.

Declan led her to a small tiled room with a sink in the corner, pumped soap and began to wash his hands and arms, stained with all manner of blood and fluids. With a glance down at his blood-speckled T-shirt, he grimaced and pulled that off too, leaving Brianna gaping at him open-mouthed.

Who knew working with horses could make a man that jacked? Declan's torso was solid muscle, he even had a perfectly defined six-pack. Brianna had to try very hard not to drool as he washed up quite unselfconsciously, wetting a cloth and wiping down those lickable abs. Finally he threw the cloth in the sink, shut off the water and leaned down to open a drawer, pulling out a towel to dry off with before turning to fix her with that dark glare again.

"Perhaps you'd now like to explain what the fuck that stunt you pulled yesterday was all about?" he growled.

I'm not afraid of you. There's a soft heart under all that growly glaring, and if I hadn't been here yesterday, hadn't seen the love in your face as you talked about your horses, I wouldn't know that. That's why.

She was wise enough not to say so, though. Instead she offered a tentative smile. "I just wanted to see the place without the red carpet being rolled out for the new owner. Wanted to see it warts and all."

"What makes you think we'd roll the red carpet out for you?" He scowled, folding his arms across his chest, which made his biceps bulge in a really distracting way. Brianna fought to keep her eyes on his face.

"I don't know that, of course," she admitted. "I just… actually, you know what? I'm feeling really stupid now because I've accidentally pissed you off, and this really wasn't the way I wanted to start off with you. Is there any chance we could start again?"

Declan's angry scowl faded away, replaced by

an expression of complete astonishment as he stared at her in silence. Finally, he unfolded his arms, held out a large hand and said "Hi. I'm Declan O'Siorain."

Finally, she knew how to pronounce his name properly! *O'Shorran*, she rehearsed mentally. "Brianna Lane," she said aloud, accepting his hand and shaking it gratefully. "It's lovely to meet you."

A spark of warmth passed through their joined hands, and Declan suddenly seemed to become aware of his half-dressed state. He jerked back, muttering "Excuse me," and hastily pulled a fleece jacket down from a rack on the wall, shrugging into it and zipping it up.

Brianna thought about making a teasing remark about enjoying the view, but she bit it back. Theirs was a fragile rapport and she didn't want to do anything to damage it. Instead, she waited until Declan had the jacket fully zipped before speaking again.

"Do you want to go check on the foal?"

"Yeah." He held the door open for her and she followed him back to the stable, where Ted and Charlie both stood outside now watching the mare and her newborn. The foal was struggling to stand on gangly legs which seemed far too long for its body, being nosed helpfully by Lansdowne Lass who was now back on her own feet.

"Fine little colt," Ted remarked to Declan as they approached. He and Charlie both gave Brianna curious stares, and Declan saved her blushes by introducing her.

"We didn't know you were coming over," Ted said in a massive understatement.

"It was an impulsive decision," Brianna admitted. "I wanted to see Galamor. I understand the Leary family have been here for generations, and it seems I'm the last one left, after my mother of course."

All three men nodded, and Charlie said unexpectedly "My father remembers your grandmother. Says she was the most beautiful girl in the west of Ireland in her day."

"Damn it, that's why I thought you looked familiar!" Declan said suddenly. "There's a painting in Alec's room. You look very like her."

Brianna smiled shyly. "I'd like to see that. Mum only had a few very old photos of her... and none from before she left Ireland. I only know what my great-uncle looked like because there were a few photos of him I found online in racing journals."

Declan's face softened further. "Alastair Leary was the finest man I'd ever known."

Ted and Charlie both nodded in complete agreement. Brianna cast her eyes down sadly.

"I wish he'd chosen to make contact before he passed away. I'd have loved to meet him."

"He was ill when he started looking for you," Declan said quietly. "By the time the agent came back to him with the report, he was bedbound. He wouldn't have wanted you to see him like that."

"He was a proud man," Ted agreed with a nod.

There was a brief, awkward silence before Charlie pushed his cap back on his grizzled head and said "It's dinnertime, Dec. Why don't you take Miss Lane up to the house and have somethin' to eat? Have Molly send a plate down for me, I'll stay with the Lass until it's time to turn in, make sure they're all right together."

Declan took a last look into the stable before nodding. The foal was nursing, his mother's head turned to nuzzle gently at her baby's flanks.

Brianna thought the pair looked absolutely perfect together, but then the foal was probably worth a small fortune, and the men were just being cautious. Ted mumbled something about checking on one of the other mares and made his escape, leaving her and Declan to return to the house together in silence.

The kitchen was bright and cheerful, Molly

bustling about serving up plates of steaming rice with what smelled like orange chicken. Declan excused himself to go get a clean shirt on, and Brianna found herself seated between a couple of the stable lads again, both of whom were eagerly stuffing their faces.

Molly's eyes were sharp, but the older woman seemed satisfied at least she and Declan were on speaking terms or Brianna wouldn't be sitting at the table. She slid a heaping plate in Brianna's direction and one of the lads poured her some lemonade.

CHAPTER EIGHT

Declan didn't taste much of his dinner, despite it being as delicious as everything else Molly cooked. He ate mechanically, hyper-aware of the young woman sitting just across the table, her head tilted to the side as she listened with interest to the anecdote young Paddy was telling her. Her laugh rang out a moment later, soft and silvery, and Declan made himself look away.

Don't get infatuated with her. She's here for her money and then she'll be gone. He stabbed his fork into a piece of chicken with unnecessary force, wincing as the tines of the fork clanked hard against the plate. Looking up again, he caught Molly giving him a reproachful stare and sighed, shoving his chair back.

"Have you finished eating, Brianna?" The plate in front of her was still half-filled, but she'd set her fork down some time ago and not touched it since. Molly's helpings were designed to fill the bellies of stable hands who'd done a hard day's work, not a pampered city miss.

A tiny voice whispered he wasn't being fair, but Declan squelched it ruthlessly. *Fair* didn't come into this. He needed to stay unemotional. Businesslike.

"Yes, thank you." Brianna cast a curious look at his barely-touched plate. "Have you?"

"I'm not hungry." He rose to his feet. "If you'd care to join me in the study… we need to talk."

She rose gracefully, smiling at young Padraig who gazed back at her adoringly. Declan gritted his teeth and gestured for her to precede him from the room.

"Please don't flirt with the staff," he said coldly as he closed the study door behind them.

Brianna whirled on him, her jaw dropping open with shock. "I beg your pardon! I was merely being friendly!"

"It's best to maintain a professional distance."

"Which is why you eat with them in the kitchen, is it?"

He flinched slightly as her accurate shot struck home. Alastair had never eaten in the kitchen, had always taken his meals in the small dining-room. In recent years, he'd insisted Declan join him there, but since the old man had died, the room seemed too quiet and lonely for Declan and he'd started eating in the kitchen again.

"We're not discussing me."

"Well, I think we should." Brianna folded her arms and stared him down. "Because I want to know who the hell you are, that my great-uncle decided to leave you half his estate."

Declan stared back at her. She had every right to ask the question, and he knew it. He blew out his cheeks with a sigh and nodded. "Please, have a seat." He gestured to the comfortable armchairs in front of the unlit fireplace. "Would you like a drink?" He crossed to the small bar built into the sideboard.

"What have you got?" Brianna eyed the whisky bottle dubiously as he picked it up and poured himself a generous shot.

"Whisky… there's gin. Sherry. Uh… brandy?"

"I'll have a brandy," she said, and he poured a measure into a snifter and handed it to her before taking a seat. She sniffed at the brandy and took a small sip before setting the glass down on a side table.

"I'm not here to fight or cause trouble," Brianna said before he could speak, surprising him again. "I know less than nothing about racehorses or horse breeding or even farming. But I do feel like my great-uncle left me half his estate for a reason, and I want to know what that is. And why he left you the other half."

Declan leaned back in his chair and took a big gulp of whisky, savouring the fiery burn as it slid down his throat. "They're questions you deserve answers to," he admitted after swallowing, "but I don't have all the answers you want, I'm afraid. I didn't know what was in the will until after it was read. Alec never discussed it with anyone but his solicitor, not that I know of."

"You had no inkling what was in it?" Brianna's gaze was intent on his face. He had difficulty meeting her eyes.

"Not really. Alec used to say I was the son he never had, so I suppose I hoped he'd leave me something, but I never expected to get half. To be honest, I thought he might leave you or your mother the lot, after he went to all that effort to find you."

Brianna leaned forward, clasping her hands on her knees. His gaze was drawn to them irresistibly, those long elegant fingers, her nails short and unpolished, which surprised him a little.

"Help me understand him, Declan. You knew him well, and it's obvious you loved him. Until a couple of weeks ago, I never even knew he existed."

He swallowed, unable to resist the earnest appeal in her eyes. He had to tell her the truth, however unpalatable it might be.

"I've known Alastair Leary all my life. My father used to own Ballybronn." He had to take another gulp of whisky, to give him the strength to talk about his father. "He was the biggest asshole in County Mayo."

Brianna's eyes widened, and her mouth formed a silent O, but she said nothing, just sat back and listened as he told her the whole sordid story.

"Alec never married, and he and my father were at odds pretty often; the two estates bordered each other and my father was a poor master who didn't bother to maintain his fences and the like. Anyway, thirty-three years ago my father came home from a visit to some American cousins with a beautiful young American bride. It didn't take long for her to learn his true colours, but she was a long way from home and anyone who might have helped her. She wore makeup to cover the bruises and soldiered on as best she could."

"I'm so sorry," Brianna said softly when

Declan paused to drain his glass. "She must have been very frightened."

"Especially once she got pregnant. He didn't even let up with the beatings then. One night, she was so afraid he'd kill her she ran away. Alastair picked her up on the road, walking in the rain, soaked through and scared out of her wits." He closed his eyes, remembering his gentle mother. "Alastair tried to get her to stay here at Galamor, or go back to America, anywhere but back to my father. Mom didn't see a way out, though, and when my father turned up with the police accusing Alastair of kidnapping her, she went back with him. He managed to keep his fists off her then until after I was born, at least. He took up another vice; gambling."

"Betting on racing?"

"And on football matches, and playing cards with cronies. Always drinking heavily and losing heavier. One night, driving home late and drunk, he hit a tree. I was two." His tone was flat as he related the story; the death of a man he didn't remember but had always hated held no importance for him. "There wasn't a will, but it turned out that didn't matter. He left nothing but debts, debts for which my mother was legally responsible. Ballybronn was twice-mortgaged. Everything had to be sold. Which is when Alastair stepped in. He bought Ballybronn and told my mother she could stay there with me as long as she wanted. He only needed the land, and he needed someone to look after the house anyway."

"He was giving her a job as well as a home," Brianna said softly.

"I don't know what would have become of Mum and I without him. I truly don't." Declan needed her to understand what kind of man Alastair Leary had been. "I was obsessed with horses before I could walk, and he took me under his wing. I dreamed of being a jockey, of course, and he encouraged me until it was obvious I was going to be too big, and then he started grooming me to follow in his footsteps. I've been helping to manage the estate since I was sixteen, and he gave me the official title of Estate Manager once I graduated - at his expense - with a degree in agricultural studies."

"You really were the son he never had," Brianna nodded, understanding. "But he never married?"

Declan gave her a crooked little smile in return. "I'm fairly sure he was in love with my mother, but she was twenty years his junior and very prejudiced against men after her terrible marriage. She looked on Alastair as a father figure and he was careful never to give her cause to think otherwise."

"Is she still alive?"

Declan winced. "Yes. But she lives in a nursing home, she has early-onset dementia. She thinks I'm my father... I can't see her any more. It's too distressing for her. I had to get Charlie to go and visit her to tell her Alec had died."

Brianna didn't seem to know what to say, and he couldn't blame her. He hadn't had a hard life, far from it; he'd grown up sheltered in the warmth of Alastair Leary's benevolent love, and the man he wished was his father in truth had left him an asset which would keep him and any descendants he might have comfortably for the rest of their lives. His family story was still a shocking one, though.

"So that's my story," he said finally, getting up to go and pour himself another whisky, "and I think I know yours, for the most part, since the dossier Alec had prepared on you was in his safe. The question now is, what are we going to do about the pickle he's landed us in?"

CHAPTER NINE

Brianna picked up her glass and took another sip of brandy to give herself time to think before she responded to Declan's question.

"Honestly, I don't quite understand why he didn't leave you everything," she admitted after a moment. "You obviously love this place; that was what I learned yesterday, over and above everything else. How much the estate and the horses mean to you."

Declan didn't meet her eyes, looking down into his glass again, but he did nod. "You've the right to it, though," he said quietly. "You're his blood heir."

"I don't even know why my grandmother left Ireland!" She threw her hands up.

"I do." He grimaced. "My father again, unfortunately. Charlie's father worked for Alec before him, and he's told me a few stories about the way my father pursued Sinead. She went to England to escape him and never came home."

"I wondered if it wasn't something like that," Brianna admitted. She smiled a little wickedly and said "But you can be assured you're not my uncle. My mother was born a little over twelve months after my grandparents arrived in Melbourne."

Declan's eyes shot back to hers, and he barked a sudden laugh. "Christ, that never even occurred to me!"

"I had thought she might have run away because she was pregnant, but my mother's date of birth didn't add up." She smiled at him. "It's probably not much comfort."

"Eh, that my father was a drunkard, a gambler and a wife-beater, but maybe not a rapist? No, not much comfort." He sounded bitter, and then he set down the glass he was holding with a sudden thud. "I don't drink normally, I should tell you."

"You've had a trying day. I think you earned one." She suspected he did everything in his power to make sure he never did anything his father had done. "I bet you don't gamble, and even though you were furious with me earlier, I don't think it even occurred to you to raise a hand against me. I was never scared, anyway."

"Good," he said gruffly. "I don't think I could

forgive myself if I ever hit a woman. And while I wouldn't say I *never* gamble, I have a strict ten-euro limit - and I only bet on *our* young 'uns."

"Of course." Brianna truly did feel safe with him. Even at the moment of fury he'd shown earlier, she didn't think violence had even occurred to him. Quietly, she took another sip of her brandy and considered her next words, but Declan spoke before she did.

"Eight million is the absolute maximum the bank will lend me, but I have the feeling it's not going to be nearly enough."

The despair on his face was evident. Brianna took a deep breath.

"Mr Connolly's preliminary assessment is the entire estate is worth something in excess of twenty-five million euros. Possibly more. He thinks one of the paintings is a Gainsborough and suggests I should get an art appraiser in, because the art collection could be worth several million on top."

"*Jaysus*." Declan buried his face in his hands.

She wasn't quite sure what to suggest. "Could the estate be split up?" she asked hesitantly. "If the art was sold, and maybe the house at Ballybronn…"

Declan shook his head. "You haven't seen the breakdown of figures." He looked up to meet her eyes. "But I'm quite sure Ballybronn isn't worth more than a million, all up. The value of the estate is in the horses, for the most part, and the revenue from the stallions. Even without Prestigious. Oracular alone is probably worth three million, but if I sold him we lose our biggest revenue stream." He chewed on his lip. "Maybe… maybe we could come to an arrangement where I pay you the eight million now and you get a share of the business profits until the rest is paid?"

"Or maybe eight million is more than I ever expected to get," Brianna said, surprising herself a little. "As I said… I think Alec should probably have left you the whole lot, anyway."

"Wait," hope dawned slowly on his face. "Are you saying you'd accept only eight million for your half? No… no, that can't be right. That's not fair. I can't let you do it." He shook his head decisively.

Brianna nibbled on a hangnail, trying to think of other options. "What if I don't sell my half at all?" she offered. "I stay in as a silent partner and I get half the profits. You draw a reasonable salary, I… get paid for not doing anything, really?"

Declan's mouth kicked up in a half-smile, and he looked at her thoughtfully. "That could work, if you don't want a lump sum. As long as you're willing to let me run things my way."

"I'm sure it's something we could work out,"

Brianna said, offering him a shy smile in return. "You see, it's a good thing I came round anonymously yesterday, because everything I saw convinced me you love this place so much you'd never do anything to put the estate at risk."

"It's the only home I've ever known," he admitted. "I hated the idea of it being left to some stranger who might sell it sight unseen. We'd be snapped up by one of the big operations who'd put their own people in charge, probably switch half the operation over to artificial insemination and over-breed the stallions, want a foal from every mare every year. I couldn't bear it."

"I understand," she said, and she really felt she did. "I'm a graphic artist and I think it's a little bit like that… when you have a creative vision, a belief yours is the right way, having someone else come in and override you and insist you make changes you can't stand, it's soul-destroying. And that's just artwork - it must be so much worse when it's living things you care about, horses and people."

Declan's expression was grateful. "You *do* understand. Bri - I'd love to work with you. Half this is rightfully yours and I promise, I'd never do anything to jeopardise any of it. I'll make sure you get your fair share, one way or another."

"And I promise I won't try to interfere with the

way you run the estate." Leaning forward, she offered her hand. "We can work out the details later, but let's shake on it, Declan. To partnership."

"To partnership," he echoed, with a genuinely delighted smile, and he reached out to grasp her hand.

A spark passed between their hands as his strong, warm fingers wrapped around hers, and in the widening of Declan's dark blue eyes, Brianna knew he'd felt it too.

"This is almost certainly a bad idea," he broke the silence first. Their hands were still clasped, their eyes locked.

"You're right," she agreed, but she didn't pull her hand away.

"Being attracted to a business partner is a recipe for disaster."

"I can't help it if you're sexy. You took your shirt off in front of me, for God's sake; this is clearly all your fault." Desperately casting about for a topic to try and break the rising tension, Brianna tried humour. Declan chortled at her remark, finally letting go of her hand.

"How about I promise to keep my shirt on in the future?"

"Too late, I already know I want to lick your abs." She gave him a cheeky grin, and he shook his head.

"You're a handful, aren't you? Isn't there some lucky guy back in Australia counting the days until you get home?"

Brianna grimaced slightly. "No. Living in the inner-city, most of the guys I meet are the metrosexual city slicker types, and honestly… that's really not my style."

"No," Declan murmured. He tilted his head and considered her. "You're not what I expected," he said frankly. "When I read the file and saw you were a graphic designer living in inner-city Melbourne, I expected some manicured society girl in sky-high heels."

"Sounds impractical and uncomfortable." Brianna looked down at her blunt nails, at the sensible hiking boots she planned to wear throughout her trip. "Especially on a farm."

"Too right." He looked morose, and she had the distinct feeling she'd touched on a nerve. Since they were being so open and honest with each other, she thought she'd ask the question.

"Sounds like prior experience talking?"

"Unfortunately." He picked up his glass, took a drink and grimaced. "I met a girl while I was at university in Dublin. Sorcha Sullivan, most beautiful girl I'd ever seen. I was besotted, and I thought she was too. Turned out a rumour somehow got started I was Alec Leary's illegitimate son and he was going to leave me the whole estate. She thought I was loaded."

Brianna winced. "How did you find out the truth?"

"I brought her down for the weekend to meet Mom and Alec. She packed only high heels to wear, refused to set foot in the yards. I knew then it wasn't going to work, no matter how blinded by lust I was. I broke it off and Sorcha fired a few parting shots about there not being enough money in the world to induce her to live in a 'hovel in the back of beyond'."

"A *hovel*?" Brianna looked around the elegantly appointed study, unable to keep in her incredulous laughter. "What a princess!"

"Alec's words exactly, except with a few more colourful ones sprinkled in." Declan smiled at her. "I wish you could have met him. You two would have got on like a house on fire."

"You'll just have to tell me all your stories. Hey… you mentioned a painting of my grandmother. Would you show it to me?"

"Of course, and then I'd best take you back to the hotel. It's getting late. Do you want to move in tomorrow?"

Startled, she blinked at him as he rose to his feet. "Move in?"

"Here, obviously. Seems a bit pointless you staying at the hotel... unless you want to, of course."

"I... suppose. Yes. If it's all right with you?"

He smiled as she stood to join him. "The Irish are famous for our hospitality, Bri, but not only that, Galamor is yours equally as much as it is mine. This is your home now, too."

"Which is very trippy," she admitted as she followed him out of the study and up the wide staircase to the first floor. "Home's never been anywhere but Melbourne."

Declan paused with his hand on the doorknob of the master suite, gazed at her earnestly. "One look at Sinead's painting and you'll understand, I hope. This place is in your blood." With that, he pushed the door open and reached to switch on the light.

Brianna had seen the room before on their tour of the house yesterday, but she hadn't noticed the painting Declan led her to stand before now. Gazing up at it, she lost her breath.

It was almost like looking in a mirror. Sinead Leary's face was a near-exact replica of her granddaughter's, right down to the elusive dimple in her chin when she smiled, a dimple Brianna had been teased endlessly about in primary school. It didn't seem to worry Sinead though as she smiled out of the painting, the green hills surrounding the lough rising in the distance, a bay horse behind her painted in out of focus. Sinead herself looked vibrantly alive, long brunette curls touched with gold in the sunshine.

"Whoever painted that was hella talented," Brianna said when she finally got her breath back.

"It was Charlie's mother, actually. Or so Charlie claims. He also says she didn't do Sinead's beauty justice… I think Charlie might had had a bit of a crush on your grandmother, back in the day. He was fourteen and she was eighteen when she went away, so he was old enough to remember her pretty well. If he'd gotten more of a look at you yesterday the jig would have been up, but he had his hands full with Prestigious in a rotten mood."

Turning from the painting, Brianna smiled at him. "What would you have done if you'd caught me out yesterday?" she asked curiously. "Just out of interest."

"Probably something unwise. At least Molly and I figured you out when you weren't here; I'd had a few hours to come to terms with it by the time you turned up this afternoon. And for the record? In your shoes, I might well have done something similar."

She gave him a grateful smile. "You've probably been nicer about it than I deserved."

He grinned, surprising her a little with the bright humour in it. "Well, you did catch me right in the middle of a foaling. I might have shouted otherwise."

"I've always had an excellent sense of timing." Brianna returned the smile, and Declan laughed aloud.

"Well, talking of timing, it's getting late, for me anyway. We start early around here. I'll take you back to the hotel now, if that's all right?"

"Oh, I can make my own way back," she disclaimed, but he flatly refused, saying the lane was far too dark and he'd be worrying about her all night. Seeing he wasn't going to give in, she finally acquiesced, and he escorted her downstairs and out to a beat-up old Land Rover.

"This is just the estate runabout," he apologized when he saw her looking at the cracked and peeling paint, the ripped upholstery. "I've got a BMW I use to get around when I need to put on a good front."

"You don't have to justify anything to me, Declan. I said I trusted you to know the business of the estate better than I do, and I meant it. I know less than nothing about running any kind of business, let alone a racehorse stud in a country on the other side of the world from my home."

In the darkness inside the vehicle, she sensed rather than saw him turn his head to look at her. He didn't say anything for a few minutes, until they were drawing up outside the hotel, and then he spoke quietly but firmly.

"If you do have anything to say, any comments about the estate or suggestions for the future, I'll listen, Brianna. I'm not going to dismiss your thoughts and opinions out of hand. Alec always listened to my 'new-fangled' ideas; we used to sit down and discuss things. I miss that."

She could hear the echo of loss in his voice, reached out impulsively to put her hand on his where it rested on the gearstick. "I'm not my great-uncle, but I'm here. I'll be happy to listen and talk things over with you whenever you want, and that includes over Skype when I go home."

"I appreciate that." He turned his hand under hers, gripped her fingers lightly. "I'll pick you up in the morning, yeah? About ten suit you?"

"Sure, that gives me time to have one of Moira's fantastic breakfasts and pack my bags. G'night!"

The last thing she heard as she slammed the door was Declan's deep chuckle. The Land-Rover's engine didn't rumble to life again until she was opening the hotel's front door, though.

CHAPTER TEN

Declan half-thought Brianna might change her mind, but she was waiting outside the hotel, perched on her suitcase and looking at her phone, when he pulled up the following morning. She looked up at the rumble of the old Land-Rover's engine and smiled.

Jesus, Mary and Joseph, he thought, *no wonder Charlie claims her grandmother was the most beautiful woman in Ireland back in the day*. Brianna's smile in the morning sunshine was spectacular.

He tried to tell himself not to look at her that way, to try and treat her professionally, like a business partner. As he hopped out of the car and picked up her suitcase to top in the back and she gave him a sunny greeting, it was extremely difficult to remember that resolution.

"Ready for some hard work? I'm gonna throw you in at the deep end," he warned as she climbed into the passenger seat.

"Good. I want to understand how the whole business works," Brianna claimed. "And I mucked out my share of stalls as a pony-obsessed teenager, I can tell you."

Declan chuckled as he started the engine again. "Eh, I'm not quite that mean. We've got ultrasounds to do today; we do them three times a week once the breeding season has started, on the mares who've been put to the stallions, to see if they've fallen pregnant or if they'll have to be mated again."

Brianna listened with apparent interest as he explained. "So the mares stay until they're definitely pregnant?" she queried.

"Yes. Like a lot of studs, we have a No Foal, No Fee policy. Mares go into oestrus every twenty-one days during the spring and summer, and stay fertile for five to eight days each time so we get quite a few shots at getting one pregnant."

She nodded, obviously filing the information away in her mind as he drove them to Galamor.

"A lot of owners send the mares to us to foal because they want to get the mare pregnant again straight away and it's not easy to safely transport a newborn foal," Declan explained as he drove.

"You said something about not liking to breed mares every year, though?"

He glanced across at her, surprised she'd remembered. "It depends on the mare. Some people treat their mares like baby factories, demanding a foal from them every year, and yes, in pure economic terms, I can understand that. A foal is worth a lot of money. However, there are a lot of studies which say, and I've observed it for myself, you get higher-quality foals if you don't force a mare to breed every year… and she'll stay healthy and fertile for longer."

The topic of conversation really wasn't helping. He'd never really equated his work with human sexuality before, but he couldn't help thinking about it as he and Brianna left the vehicle and walked to the specially outfitted stall where Ted conducted the ultrasounds. Especially since she was wearing those tight jeans again, outlining the shape of her ass, drawing his eyes to the way her hips rolled as she walked.

Stop looking at her ass, you pervert! She'd slap your face if she caught you.

Except maybe she wouldn't. She'd teased back in the study last night, saying she'd wanted to *lick his abs*, of all things, when he took his shirt off to wash up after the foaling.

"Morning," Ted said cheerfully as they entered the room. "I understand Declan's planning to teach you the business from the inside, Brianna."

"Something like that." She gave the vet the same sunny smile she'd favoured Declan with earlier, and he mentally kicked himself for thinking he'd been getting special favour from her.

"Well, we'll start with taking a look at Coral Diva's insides, hm." Ted nodded to the mare one of the stable lads was leading in. "Come stand over here with me and I'll explain what we're seeing on the screen."

Brianna was genuinely interested in the process Ted was explaining to her, but she was struggling to concentrate. She was too hyper-aware of Declan, standing at the mare's head and talking to her in soothing tones, stroking her nose and keeping her quiet as the vet worked. His voice was low, his Irish accent making the words he was crooning sing-song and hypnotic. The mare seemed to love it, her entire attention focussed on Declan even as Ted pressed the ultrasound head against her sensitive belly.

"Damn," Ted murmured, drawing Brianna's attention back to the screen. "Look at that."

"What am I looking at?" It was all just blurry shades of grey, to her.

"Here." Ted's left hand pointed at the screen. "And here."

"They look the same…"

"Exactly. She's carrying twins."

"That's not a good thing, I take it?" His tone told her so, as well as Declan's frown, though Declan never stopped his petting and crooning to the mare. "Surely two foals should be a great outcome, in terms of value?"

"In theory, yes, but equine twin pregnancies don't usually turn out well. Statistically the chance of a live foal from a twin pregnancy is less than 20%, and the outlook for future pregnancies isn't good either. Coral Diva's only eight, she could have plenty more foals."

"So… what happens now?" Those odds didn't sound good.

Ted didn't answer for a moment, clicking the trackball on the ultrasound machine to mark spots and taking measurements. "I attempt a selective termination," he responded finally. "It's a standard procedure. Then we do another ultrasound in a couple days to make sure she's still pregnant with the one. Here, I'm going to need you to hold this steady right here so I can see what I'm doing as I introduce the instrument."

Brianna wasn't quite sure at how she felt assisting in what was effectively a partial abortion, but then she supposed Declan and Ted were probably both Catholic and they seemed to view this as a routine procedure. She asked a few more questions about twin pregnancies in horses and Ted answered absently as he worked.

"Thoroughbreds are quite prone to twin pregnancies," Declan answered one question when Ted was too absorbed. "More so than pony breeds. Before we routinely started doing ultrasounds, we used to lose foals and even mares every year because of difficult twin births. It's much safer for the mare to make sure she doesn't carry twins."

"There we go," Ted murmured, watching the ultrasound screen. "That's got it. All right, there's a good girl." He patted the mare's flank gently as he removed his instrument and took it to the steriliser on the other side of the room, pulling off his surgical gloves to discard them. "I'll put her on the scan schedule for Tuesday, Declan, to check the single embryo is still in place."

Brianna watched as Declan handed the mare off to her stable lad to lead out. Declan came to stand by her, still holding the ultrasound head in her hand, and put one of his hands lightly on her shoulder.

"You okay? That was a little confronting for your first day."

"Yeah," she looked up at him, her brow furrowed slightly with concern. "I guess… I didn't realize this was something so routine. Especially in Catholic Ireland, it feels… odd."

"Believe me, nobody would be this sanguine if it were human life we were talking about here," Declan's expression was understanding. "I can show you all the facts and statistics to back up our reasoning, if you want."

"No, no. I trust you wouldn't be doing this if it wasn't the right thing to do. After all, that foal would be worth a lot of money, wouldn't it?"

"At least a hundred thousand euros," Declan agreed, "but the odds of both of them being born alive would be extremely low. The remaining foal now has a much higher chance of survival."

Another mare came clopping into the ultrasound stall and Declan squeezed Brianna's shoulder gently. "We have to do this in about five to ten percent of cases," he said quietly. "If you don't want to be here for the next one, that's fine. There are lots of other things to do, I just thought you might find this interesting."

"I do." Reaching up her free hand, she pressed her fingers against his. "It's fine, Declan, really. Now I know it's the best thing for all concerned, I'm okay with it."

"Good. Believe me, I wish it wasn't. I wish we could let twins be born as often as they're conceived." He smiled at her, his eyes warm, and once again she felt that connection between them in the brush of their fingers, and she knew from the way his pupils flared wide he was feeling it too.

Taking a deep breath, she tore her eyes away by sheer effort of will, and blushed scarlet as she met Ted's eyes. The vet was giving them an extremely interested look, his eyebrows raised, though he didn't say anything as Brianna took a quick step away from Declan.

You don't need everyone gossiping about you. No matter how sexy he is, you need to keep your distance.

Declan had obviously spotted Ted's inquisitive stare as well, because he shot a quick scowl in the vet's direction before going to take the mare from her handler. "Let's get this done," he said crisply. "We've got eight more waiting after this one. If we don't get cracking none of us are going to get any lunch."

CHAPTER ELEVEN

They were too busy for Ted to say anything to Declan until the last mare had been scanned and led out. Brianna asked blushingly where the bathroom was and Declan directed her to the small washroom block at the end of the row of stalls. Cleaning and putting away the ultrasound machine, Ted turned and gave Declan an expressive look.

"Don't say anything," Declan warned.

"Do I really need to?"

"No, you really don't."

"Good." Ted closed the cupboard door with a firm thud. "Brianna's a nice lass. She deserves your respect, and the respect of the lads. They won't give it if they think you're sleeping with her."

"I daresay you're going to explode when I tell you she's moving into Galamor today?"

Ted dropped his clipboard. "Are you kidding me?"

Declan winced at his friend's incredulous look. He'd known Ted a long time; the vet had moved to the area and married Molly when Declan was only a kid. The disappointed, shocked look on Ted's face really stung. "There's nothing in it, I swear. It just seems silly for her to be staying at the hotel - wrong, in fact! She has as much right to Galamor as I do; more, by blood! Alastair would take my head off if I didn't invite her to stay in the house."

"The point is she'll be staying in the house *with you*," Ted said dryly. "And while it's a hive of activity during the day, by night it'll be just the two of you. You know what the gossips will say; that you're living in sin."

"She's only here for a couple of weeks!" Declan scrubbed a hand through his hair. "God damn it, this is ridiculous, there's nothing going on!"

"That'd be a lot more believable if the pair of you weren't making calf eyes at each other." Ted raised a sardonic eyebrow. "Maybe Molly and I should move in too. Just while she's here."

"I guess it's that or I go sleep in the stables,"

Declan grumbled. "This is ridiculous. It's the new millennium, not the nineteenth century!"

"This is Catholic Ireland, Dec. In some ways, we still *are* in the nineteenth century." Ted flashed a sudden, mischievous smile. "You could always marry her. Solve all your problems at once, that would!"

"Don't be ridiculous," Declan scoffed, following Ted as they left the building, but the seed of an idea had been planted and he couldn't stop thinking about it as they walked along the stable block to rejoin Brianna. Marrying her would resolve all of the issues with the inheritance, after all. He wouldn't have to worry about bank loans or profit sharing; he could plough all the profits back into the estate, expand the stallion barn, buy more land and make Leary Estates the finest stud farm in Ireland...

You're being ridiculous. You barely know her. He tried to shake the thought loose, but as they sat in Galamor's kitchen and ate sandwiches with the stable hands, he couldn't stop looking at Brianna. She was everything a man like him could want in a wife, really; she was smart, she was pretty and she loved horses, and that was even before he started thinking about the financial benefits.

The financial side of things was why it would

be a bad idea for him to even try to court her, of course. She'd never believe he wasn't pursuing her because of the money, and he wasn't even sure of his own motives in the matter, if he was going to be honest with himself. Yes, he'd been attracted to her from the moment she stepped out of Liam Connolly's car, long before he had any inkling she was Alastair's heir. There'd been an undeniable spark between them even then, and he was pretty sure Brianna was attracted to him too.

She looked across the table at that moment and smiled at him, pure unfettered joy in her expression, and Declan's heart thumped hard in his chest.

He hadn't felt like this in a long time, he recognized dimly as he smiled back at Brianna helplessly. Not since Sorcha, the object of his youthful adoration, had a woman captured his attention in such a way. Brianna was a very different woman to his old crush, though; she might have come halfway around the world to be here, but she was obviously perfectly comfortable in the countryside.

"What's the plan for this afternoon, Declan?" she asked, jerking him out of his reverie.

"We've got a few departures going out," he said, after taking a moment to gather his thoughts. "Mares that are confirmed pregnant, and they're being collected to return to their usual stables. I like to supervise them going out, and we've a couple more coming in for a late-season breeding. We'll get them settled in."

"Or you're welcome to come with me," Ted chirped up. "I'm going to check on the new foal you saw born yesterday, and then I've got a round of deworming to do on the older foals who've reached eight weeks of age. Could use an extra pair of hands."

Brianna looked from Declan to Ted and back again, indecision clear on her face. Declan clenched his hands under the table, willing himself to remain quiet, to leave the choice to her. Surely she'd enjoy going with Ted more, handling the foals...

"I'll go with you, Declan, if you don't mind. If Ted can find someone else to help him?" she said hesitantly.

"Plenty of willing hands," Ted said cheerfully.

Declan tried to wipe the inane grin off his face as Ted's sharp eyes fell on him, but he knew from the way Ted rolled his eyes he was failing miserably. He was acting like a teenage boy with his first crush... and right at that moment, he couldn't care less.

Lunch finished, they headed out to see to the mares departing that afternoon. All three were returning to the same stable, and the truck to collect them had already arrived, the head groom from their usual home checking over his charges with experienced hands.

"They're looking well, Declan," the groom said, straightening up as he saw Declan approaching with Brianna. "You've obviously taken good care of them."

"Of course," Declan said with amusement in his tone. "That's why your owners won't send their mares anywhere else. That, and Fandingus won three out of five so far this spring. Fandingus is this beautiful mare's last foal by Prestigious," he told Brianna, reaching to stroke one mare's dark head. "Racing in his first season, and it's obvious he's going to be a star."

"So she's been put back to Prestigious again?" Brianna asked, holding her hand out for the mare to sniff delicately before stroking her soft nose.

"Boss says he's the best value for money stallion in Ireland," the groom nodded to her. "You visiting, miss?"

"This is Brianna Lane, Alastair's great-niece," Declan introduced her. "Half-owner of the estate. She's staying for a while to learn about the business. Brianna, this is Joe Collins, the best horse handler in Ireland. I keep trying to hire him but he has an unaccountable loyalty to his current employer."

"It's not unaccountable at all. He pays well."

Brianna chuckled at that, and Joe gave her a grin. "Nice t'meet you, Miss Lane. I'll get my ladies loaded and be off, then. Get them home in time for their supper."

"You have all the paperwork?" Declan checked everything was in order, and when Joe acquiesced, guided Brianna to one side where they could observe the four mares being carefully loaded into the big horse truck.

Brianna could see how well the mares were cared for, legs and tails bandaged in case of bumps on the journey, light summer rugs protecting their glossy coats, hay tied up in nets for them to graze as they travelled. "More comfortable than an international plane flight," she said laughingly to Declan, who grinned in response.

"You're not wrong there. I flew to America last year on Alastair's behalf to look at some mares he wanted to consider, and I was in cattle class. Those seats aren't built for big men."

She could imagine how uncomfortable he would have been, long legs wedged up against the seat in front, broad frame compressed by the narrow seats. Nodding in sympathy, she waved a farewell to Joe as the groom secured the tailgate and touched his cap to them before heading around to hop into the driver's side of the truck. "Huh - somehow I thought he'd travel in the back with them."

"It's neither safe nor legal to ride in the back of a horse truck," Declan informed her. "Joe drives so he can ensure they get the smoothest ride. Got to take good care of those pregnant girls."

Brianna smiled at him. "The horses here are so pampered and protected - would that pregnant women got such tender care!"

"They would here, for sure," Declan said immediately. "I'd probably be the worst expectant father in the world, hovering all the time. My wife would be locking me out of the house to keep me out of her hair."

She laughed… but she also found herself thinking about what it would be like to be married to Declan. To have his attention focussed entirely on her, have those strong, yet gentle hands touching her, caressing her.

Don't go there, Bri. Declan already agreed with you that acting on this attraction is a bad idea. Don't go building up impossible fantasies in your head.

The problem was, she'd always had a vivid imagination. It was an asset as a graphic designer, but right now her mind's eye was showing her Declan as a father, holding a dark-eyed child as he set them tenderly on the back of their first pony.

"Brianna," Declan said, and she jerked herself out of her daydream. He was looking at her oddly. "Are you all right? You were a thousand miles away. Penny for your thoughts."

She couldn't exactly tell him she'd been imagining him as a devoted father to their children, so she smiled and said "Just taking it all in. There's a lot to learn."

"That there is. Come on. We'll go make sure the stables are prepared for our new arrivals - they're due any minute!"

CHAPTER TWELVE

By the time they entered the house for dinner, Brianna was exhausted, and she'd done little more than tag around after Declan all day. She was too accustomed to spending her workday at her desk, rather than on her feet; she'd need to build up her stamina. No wonder Declan was so lean and fit, she thought as she flopped into a chair at the dinner table. He'd never stopped moving, and he'd done plenty of physical work as well, stepping in a couple of times to handle recalcitrant horses, including one memorable visit to the stallion barn where a mare had taken exception to the stallion brought in to service her.

"You all right?" Declan smiled warmly at her

across the table as he took his own seat, and she gave him a tired smile.

"Yes, but I think I'll be turning in early tonight. At the moment I feel like I could fall asleep face down on this table."

Molly was dishing up a thick, savoury stew tonight, served with hunks of crusty bread smeared with fresh butter. Brianna felt almost too tired to eat, but after the first mouthful she realized how hungry she was and tucked in.

"I'll put Ted's plate in the oven," Molly said loudly. "He's just over at the house packing a bag for us."

"Where're you off too, Moll?" one of the stable lads piped up.

"Ted and I are moving in to the big house here while Miss Lane is visiting."

"Why?" came the innocent question. Brianna met Declan's eyes with the same question, saw his amusement before he inclined his head towards Molly.

"Because I'll not have any gossip about Miss Lane's reputation, what with her staying under Declan's roof." Molly clipped the stable lad's ear gently as she passed.

The lad's eyes slid to Brianna, and she saw his bemusement. She shared it.

"Nobody's going to gossip about Brianna, Moll," Declan said firmly. "Not if they want to keep working for me, anyway."

Molly's mouth firmed into a tight line. "Not all the folks as might talk work for you, Declan O'Siorain. I've put Miss Lane in the room at the end of the hallway and Ted and I will take the one next door."

Brianna tried not to laugh. "Molly, really, you don't need to do that. I don't need a chaperone. And I'll be going back home in a couple of weeks anyway; I'm really not too worried if some small-minded people want to gossip. Frankly, they'd make it up anyway if they wanted to, whether you're staying here or not. Please don't put yourself and Ted out for my sake."

Molly considered her thoughtfully, glancing at Declan briefly before finally shrugging. "Well. If you're sure."

"I'm sure. Tell Ted to quit packing and come get his dinner. It's wonderful, by the way. It's a good thing I'm doing plenty of exercise or none of my clothes will fit by the time I go home!"

*   *   *

Declan watched in admiration as Brianna

charmed Molly into doing things her way; she had the older woman wrapped around her little finger, he thought, just like the stable lads who hung on her every word. After dinner, she insisted on helping clean up, refusing to let Molly lift a finger, and firmly chivvied Molly and Ted out of the house after the others.

Closing the door behind them, she turned to grin at him. "I feel like a teenager again, desperate for her parents to go out so she can get up to mischief."

"What mischief did you have in mind?" He raised his brows at her.

Chuckling, Brianna shook her head. "Even if I had anything in mind, I'm wrecked. The only thing I want is a long hot bath."

"I'll show you up to your room."

Her bags were sitting in the front hallway; Declan scooped them up easily in passing and there was nothing left for Brianna to do but follow him up the stairs, trying not to gaze at his ass in the process, or the way his muscles shifted under his close-fitting T-shirt.

Declan led her to the end of the landing and opened the door to a large, airy room she remembered from her tour of the house. With yellow and white striped wallpaper and a white bedcover patterned with tiny yellow flowers, the room seemed full of sunshine even at night.

"This is so lovely, thank you," she said as Declan set her bags at the foot of the bed and turned back to her, smiling.

"No problem. Don't feel like you're a guest here, Brianna… this house is half yours, remember! Treat it like your own home, please."

"What, lounging about in old sweatpants and drinking orange juice straight from the carton?" she said mischievously, making him laugh.

"You're totally welcome to do the first, but you'd better make sure Molly doesn't catch you doing anything like the second in *her* kitchen."

"I wouldn't dare touch anything in there. Is there somewhere I can make coffee before going downstairs in the morning, though? I'm not really fit to be seen until I've had a cup."

"I make my own in my room," Declan admitted. "I could move the machine somewhere you can access it too… there's a small open area at the bend in the landing that's never really been used for anything. I could put a small table and a couple chairs there, it can be our coffee nook. There's a bathroom right next to it to grab water."

"Sounds wonderful, but I don't want to put you to any trouble," Brianna said hesitantly.

"No trouble at all. You settle in, unpack, have a bath. I'll go scrounge around the attic. There are several pieces of furniture up there which might do." With a parting grin, he left her alone, closing the door behind him.

"Stop being so nice, goddamnit," Brianna muttered at the closed door. "It's making it really hard not to lust after you." With a sigh, she headed for the bathroom door. Time to get the bath running - in a magnificent claw-footed bathtub she was dying to try out - and then start her unpacking.

After a long, luxurious soak - there were even lavender bath salts in a small dish on the vanity she made good use of - Brianna pulled on the T-shirt and shorts she'd been wearing as pyjamas and opened her bedroom door. It was only eight o'clock, too early to go to bed. She wondered if Declan was in his study, or maybe in the TV room downstairs. Hesitantly, she made her way along the landing towards the stairs, pausing as she passed a small table which hadn't been there before, a capsule coffee machine set atop it with a box of capsules and a pair of upturned mugs.

"That man's a keeper," she murmured to herself, and screamed with shock when the man himself said;

"Well, thank you," just behind her.

"Don't do that!" Brianna almost wailed, clutching at her heart.

"Sorry! I thought you'd seen my door open," he gestured to the door across the landing. "I was bringing my small fridge out, so we can both use the milk in our coffee."

"I stand by my words about you being a keeper," she said as her pulse slowed, watching him muscle a small bar fridge out of his room and park it by the table before grabbing the cable and plugging it in.

Declan grinned. "Just don't steal my beer, not that I have much of it."

"You're safe there. I've never liked the stuff."

He straightened up, close to her, way more in her space than she normally liked people to get, but she had no urge to step back. His eyes darkened, his gaze falling to her lips, the silence suddenly humming with tension.

"We already decided this was a bad idea, didn't we," Brianna said after a long, breathless moment.

"Yeah, but I can't remember why." He was staring at her as though he wanted to eat her up, and she absolutely wanted him to. She swayed towards him, closing the last small space between them, and reached up to put her arms around his neck.

The first kiss was light, a bare brush of lips, but

that didn't satisfy either of them for more than a second.

CHAPTER THIRTEEN

Declan's strong hands curved under Brianna's ass and lifted, bringing her up to his level so he could kiss her more easily. She immediately wrapped her legs around his waist and her arms around his neck, kissing him back fervently. Carrying her easily, he turned to enter his bedroom, taking her over to the bed and laying her down, finally breaking the kiss to look into her eyes.

"You sure?" he asked thickly.

For answer, Brianna pulled at his T-shirt, trying to drag it off over his head. Declan smiled and reached up to help her, throwing the unwanted garment aside and smiling in pure masculine satisfaction as she surveyed his broad shoulders and thickly muscled chest appreciatively.

"Gorgeous," Brianna sighed appreciatively, reaching up to trace the dips and hollows of his torso with her fingertips, feeling the coarse texture of his dark brown chest hair, following it as it narrowed to a fine happy trail down the centre of his muscled abs.

He'd changed out of his jeans to a pair of old sweatpants after showering, and there was only worn, loose elastic to pluck out of the way before her fingers encountered smooth, hard heat. Declan hissed as her hand closed around his already-erect cock, said her name hoarsely before his mouth sought hers again, hungry and eager.

Declan let her take the lead, his hands exploring lightly over her clothes until she reared back impatiently and dragged off her T-shirt, flinging it away and smiling at the look on his face as he gazed at her freed breasts. She'd always been curvaceous, was proud of her naturally high and round breasts, and he made it more than clear he very much appreciated her curves as he reached out to cup her breasts reverently in his big hands, full flesh almost overflowing.

"You are *glorious*," he murmured, before bending his head to worship her with his mouth, suckling pale pink nipples into pouting, strawberry-red peaks, taking his time to arouse her thoroughly until she was moaning and squirming under him on the bed, her fingers scraping at his scalp as she held his head to her breast.

Finally satisfied with the state of mindless arousal he'd coaxed from her, Declan abandoned her breasts to kiss downwards across her stomach, fingers lightly easing the waistband of her shorts down. "This okay?" he asked quietly, kissing lower.

"Oh hell yes," Brianna said immediately, opening her eyes to look down at him. His dark blue eyes gleamed up at her as he chuckled quietly, pulling her shorts lower. She pressed her heels into the mattress to lift her hips obligingly for him to remove them completely, thinking how glad she was she'd looked on this trip as a holiday, and gone for a wax before leaving Melbourne.

"Fuuuck," Declan whispered, gazing at the thin landing strip of her Brazilian waxed pussy. "Oh fuck, that's so hot."

He didn't sleep around much, despite the way he looked, Brianna found herself thinking. Surely even girls in the rural west of Ireland got Brazilian waxes. Grinning, she lifted a foot to hook it over his shoulder, pressing her heel against his back to urge him closer.

"Come and get a closer look."

"I want to do more than look, I want to taste." He kept his eyes on hers, waiting for her nod of permission before he dived in, making his tongue into a point and flicking it lightly over her clit.

Brianna shuddered, bending her knees and setting her feet flat on the mattress, opening herself wide up for Declan's exploration. He settled comfortably on his stomach, arms curling around her thighs to hold her still while his mouth drove her absolutely crazy.

He didn't come up for air until she climaxed, squealing her ecstasy without care for how loud she might be.

"Good think you convinced Molly not to stay over," Declan murmured, kissing his way back up her stomach.

"Especially since you didn't even close the door," Brianna gasped out in response. Declan jerked around to look and then laughed.

"Jaysus, you're right. Don't worry, nobody ever comes into the house in the evenings. They give me my privacy."

"Good thing too." She was still breathing fast, her skin quivering wherever Declan touched her. He placed warm, light kisses over her breasts, spiralling in towards her nipples, giving each one in turn a quick lick. She hummed with pleasure, stroking his hair, feeling the crisp texture of his curls, the slight shagginess at the nape of his neck where it really needed a trim. Teasingly, she tugged gently.

"Growing a mullet?"

"Jaysus, no way!" He pulled back with a horrified look. "Is it getting that long?"

"It's not so bad." She giggled at his expression. "I could cut it for you, if you like. I did school work experience at a hairdresser, picked up a few tricks."

"Sure. I never seem to get the time, otherwise." He rested his chin between her breasts and gave her a soulful look. "Poor overworked Declan."

"You love it, don't give me that." Brianna snorted. "You're a workaholic."

"I'm not so sure about that… you know the saying about finding something you love to do, and then finding a sucker to pay you to do it? That's me. I'm doing something I love, I'd gladly do for free and I… well, Alastair used to pay me very well to do it. Now it's half mine and I know every drop of blood, sweat and tears I put in…" he trailed off, apparently unable to put his feelings into words.

"You're lucky," Brianna said quietly, stroking her fingers through his curly hair. He grinned at her, a glint coming back into his dark blue eyes.

"I'm feeling pretty lucky right now."

She laughed. "Well, technically, you didn't get lucky *yet*. Get your pants off and we'll fix that."

"Yeah... about that. I don't have any condoms." His grimace was a little rueful. "It's... been a while."

"And I didn't bring any with me. Didn't expect to find out my partner in this enterprise was a studly Irish sex god." She smiled at him, deliberately keeping her tone light. "I am on the Pill, though. So sex is still an option."

The look of hunger on his face was unmistakable. "If you're sure?"

The heat starting to build again in her core made the idea too tempting to resist. Deliberately, she nudged the back of his sweatpants down an inch or so with her heel. "Get these off. I want to see what I'm getting."

Declan pulled back off her and knelt upright, pushing the sweatpants down to his knees before kicking out of them completely. Brianna stared hungrily as the rest of his body was revealed to her; narrow waist and lean hips tapering out to the powerfully muscular thighs of a horseman. His cock, jutting proudly from a nest of dark brown curls, was perfectly in proportion to his tall, solid form.

"Oh, *yummy*," she said on a soft exhale,

making him laugh. Eyes on her face, he wrapped his hand around the base of his cock and pumped a few times, showing her he hadn't even quite been at full arousal as he thickened and lengthened further.

"How do you like it?" Declan asked in a soft growl.

Brianna gulped, licked her lips. "Slow to start, then hard and fast," she confessed in a near-whisper. "A real pounding, to finish."

"Jesus, Mary and Joseph, you'll be the death of me," Declan pretended to clutch at his heart. "But I'll die a happy man!"

Brianna giggled as he fell on her, the tension of the moment broken by his teasing, and opened her arms to him. Hooking her legs up around his lean hips, she sucked in her breath as the thick, hot tip of his cock nudged against her pussy.

"Oh God, that feels good," she moaned. "Yes... please, more!"

"Slow and steady to start, remember?" He sought her lips for a kiss as his hips rocked slowly. "Holy Mother, you're so tight."

She could only moan, high-pitched, frantic sounds as he slid slowly inside her, soaked pussy welcoming his intrusion even though it was definitely a stretch for her. It felt amazing, Declan taking it slow, kissing her jaw and throat as he eased deeper, his chest hair a sensual rasp against her aching nipples. She clutched at his broad shoulders, short nails digging in hard as she panted for breath.

"Okay?" Declan checked, and Brianna nodded frantically, rolling her hips, trying to get the friction she so desperately needed.

"Please," she whimpered, and he chuckled hoarsely.

"Beautiful woman. I got you." He shifted back on his heels, firm hands on her ass lifting her up into his lap, her back arched, shoulders still down on the mattress. The change in angle had her seeing stars.

"Oh God, yes!"

Declan seemed unable to find words, just making harsh sounds in his throat as his hips began to thrust, slamming roughly back and forth, his cock shuttling in and out hard, giving Brianna exactly what she needed. Her shrieks of ecstasy would surely have brought anyone in the house running, but they were quite alone. Declan's deep roar of triumph followed shortly afterwards, and then there was only the sound of rapid breathing, slowing gradually as they lay side by side on the bed, Declan's face buried in Brianna's hair as he held her close.

CHAPTER FOURTEEN

Brianna woke alone, wrapped snugly in a nest of blankets. The indentation made by Declan's head on the other pillow was cool to the touch, so she knew he'd been gone a while. He was probably a dawn riser, she realised, untucking herself from the blankets and wincing slightly as her thighs protested the movement.

There was a clock on the bedside table, the display reading 6:51. Stretching luxuriantly, she couldn't keep the smile from her lips at the pleasurable aches all over her body.

They'd made love a second time before falling asleep, and then once more during the night when she woke and went to get a drink, only to find him awake on her return to the bed. She rode him that time, mounting up and smiling down at him as his hands reached up to cup her breasts, thumbs teasing her nipples.

All in all, it was the best night of sex Brianna had ever experienced. Aching in every limb, she headed back to her own room for a long, hot shower to wash the scent of sex off her body.

Molly was in the kitchen when she made her way downstairs, pulling fresh loaves of bread from the big stove. The delicious scent set Brianna's mouth watering.

"Oh God, that smells good," she almost moaned.

Molly smiled, waved an oven mitt in her direction. "Sit down, sit down. These are too hot, but they'll cool quickly, and I've got bacon in the warming oven. How do you like your eggs?"

"Infrequently," Brianna said with an apologetic smile. "They don't agree with me particularly, I'm afraid. Just bacon with some of that bread will be fantastic."

"Coffee?" Molly offered hospitably.

"I already had a cup upstairs, but I'd love another one. I'll make it, though. Just tell me where to find stuff. I certainly don't expect you to wait on me, Molly!"

Molly turned to look at her fully then, beaming, though her expression quickly darkened. "Oh, that boy," she sighed.

Brianna's brow furrowed in confusion. "I beg your pardon?"

"You've got your grandmother's fair Irish skin, Brianna Lane. Shows stubble rash something terrible." Molly shook her head reproachfully.

Brianna's fair skin showed her blush far too well too. She refused to duck her head and look ashamed, though, keeping her eyes firmly on Molly's face. "And that is nobody's business but Declan's and mine."

"I hear you." Molly sighed as she turned away, going over to a large coffee machine in the corner of the kitchen. "If you don't want to put up with a lot of nudging and winking behind your back when you go out to the yards, though, you'll take a minute or so to put on a little makeup first."

"That I can do," Brianna agreed, going to see what Molly was up to. The older woman stood back and let her operate the coffee machine, watching with an eagle eye until it was apparent Brianna had the hang of it.

"It's not my business," Molly said, busy at the stove as Brianna sat down with her coffee cup, "but how long do you plan to stay?"

"I don't know," Brianna admitted. "I have an open-ended return ticket, so there's no definite date for my flight back, though my original plan was to stay for two weeks or so. I have up to four weeks' paid leave from work, as long as I keep up with my current projects via email. After that, I'd have to talk to my boss, see what could be worked out."

Molly's gaze was direct. "You should stay."

"Please don't tell me I have to marry Declan now I've slept with him." Brianna laughed, trying to break the tension. Molly didn't smile.

"And why not?"

"Because we hardly know each other!"

"Didn't stop you from rolling around between the sheets, now did it?" Molly put a plate down on the table with a couple of crusty, still-steaming bread rolls and a stack of crispy bacon.

"That's different!" Brianna bit her lip as Molly gave her an old-fashioned look. She wasn't going to convince the country Irishwoman that hooking up with Declan was just sex. Privately, she admitted, it *wasn't* just sex, not for her at any rate. She wasn't ready to put a name to exactly what it was quite yet, but she was already thinking about how she might be able to convince her boss to extend her leave, or give her more projects she could work on remotely.

"Do you know where Declan would be?" Brianna asked once she'd made short work of her breakfast.

Molly gave her a knowing look, but said only "Take a walk down to the main yards, anyone will be able to point you to him. He makes his presence felt."

Walking out of the house, she didn't even have to look; Declan was standing only a few steps away, hands on lean hips as he watched a stable lad lead a mare up and down the driveway, a long-legged foal dancing at her heels.

"Good morning." Brianna moved up to stand alongside him, and he glanced sideways to give her a broad smile.

"It is now."

She smiled back and suppressed the urge to move closer, to touch him. "What are we looking at?"

"A very expensive mare from France whose name I can't even get close to pronouncing." Declan grinned down at her. "And her equally expensive and even more unpronounceable foal, who is already demonstrating his desire to be a future steeplechaser. He jumped clean out over the stable door this morning in his eagerness to get out to the pastures. Landing on the hard concrete of the yard didn't go so well for him, though. Just having a look to check he hasn't done himself any serious damage."

"Ouch." Brianna turned back to look at the foal, all gangling legs and flying hooves as he tried to duck his head under his mother's belly to get a drink of milk mid-trot. The mare nudged him away, and the foal skittered forward and tried to nip the stable lad, who fended him off with the ease of long practice. "He looks like a troublemaker."

"Yes, and his dam hasn't gone into season on schedule." Declan nodded to the stable lad. "I think he's all right, Eamon. Take them to the paddock and I'll have Ted check up on him tonight."

The stable lad touched his forelock respectfully and led the mare away, skilfully evading the foal's teeth again.

"I guess there's no such thing as an everyday routine here," Brianna said thoughtfully as they walked towards the main stable yard.

"I don't know about that." Declan's hand brushed hers, fingers curling to hold her hand for a moment before he seemed to think better of it and let go. "We try to keep the routine for the horses as consistent as possible - they do best with regular feeding times and so on. But yes, every day brings new challenges. My job's never boring, that's for sure!"

"What's on the agenda for today, then?" she asked.

"I thought you might like to go for a ride."

Brianna's head snapped around. Declan grinned at her reaction.

"Yes, we do have riding horses here," he anticipated her question. "I'm back and forth between Galamor and Ballybronn several times a day some days, and starting the car just to drive that distance seems a waste of fuel. Riding over gives me time to think, as well as enabling me to look over the fences and the stock." He was leading her into a smaller side yard, where two horses were saddled and waiting, tied up to a rail.

"I'm not really dressed for this," Brianna thought to say, glancing down at her jeans and hiking boots.

"You'll do well enough. We won't gallop. Not today, at any rate." Declan's grin was mischievous. "Ever ridden an ex-racehorse before?"

She eyed the long-legged pair of bay thoroughbreds nervously. "No, I haven't."

"They're well trained, don't worry. A friend of mine runs a programme called Racehorse Rehab, designed to take retired racehorses - non-breeding stock - at the end of their racing careers, and retrain them for riding horses."

"Nice idea," Brianna approved. "So who are these two? And which one's mine?"

"Either." Declan shrugged amiably. "They both have long fancy official names, but here we call them Shadow and Tigger."

"Tigger sounds as though he might be a bit bouncy for me. I'll take Shadow."

Declan chuckled at her joke and handed her a couple of dried apple slices from his pocket, so she could introduce herself to Shadow properly. Five minutes later they were mounted up and riding out of the yard, heading along the lakeshore towards Ballybronn.

Brianna found herself riveted by the beauty of the view, the deep blue of the lake and the rich green of the hills on the other side, just a few wide clouds scudding by high in the sky. A lazy breeze touched a few small ripples on the lake,

"I take this for granted," Declan's quiet voice interrupted her reverie. "Seeing your expression, though, makes me look at it with new eyes."

"I'm not sure I've ever seen anywhere as beautiful as this," Brianna said honestly. "Nor anywhere so *green*."

"It hasn't rained since you got here, but we get plenty, even in the summer. Doesn't it rain in

Melbourne? I know they call Australia the dry continent, but I had the impression Melbourne was in the south and had proper seasons?"

"We do." Brianna laughed to herself. "Four seasons in one day, sometimes. One day last winter I got sunburned and bruised from a hailstorm on the same day."

Declan looked incredulously at her, sure she had to be pulling his leg. She grinned back at him. "I'm serious. We have seasons, but they're not the same as what you have here - they're reversed, for starters. Christmas is a time for barbecues and beach parties, not snow and ice!"

CHAPTER FIFTEEN

They spent the whole day in each other's company, talking and laughing, utterly comfortable together like people who'd known each other for years instead of days. And that evening, once they were finally alone, Declan pulled Brianna into his arms and kissed her like a starving man.

"I've been wanting to do that all damn day," he gritted out, pupils dilated with lust as he gazed down at her. "Come to bed. I want to kiss every inch of that delectable body of yours."

They ran laughing hand in hand up the stairs like a pair of kids, but there was nothing childish about the way Declan touched her, the feelings he aroused in her. She responded in kind, almost ripping his shirt in her eagerness to get it off, pushing him down to the mattress and straddling his body, grinding down on him with a guttural moan of pleasure.

Neither of them lasted more than a minute, Brianna toppling off Declan to collapse to the bed with a groan.

"This isn't going to do my sore hips any good," she mumbled, face-down in the pillows.

Chuckling, he rolled to straddle her thighs, strong hands digging into her buttocks and the backs of her thighs to knead and massage the sore muscles she was nursing after being on a horse again for the first time in several years.

Brianna moaned shamelessly as Declan massaged her aches away, completing the job of thoroughly relaxing her he'd started with that magnificent orgasm. "I'm beginning to think Molly's right," she mumbled vaguely.

"She usually is, but what was it about this time?"

She couldn't exactly tell him Molly had suggested she stay and marry Declan, so instead she said "Just that you were a keeper."

Declan laughed fondly. "Bless her. I'm surprised she didn't tell you to put a ring on it."

Brianna's silence must have given her away,

because he stilled for a moment before resuming his massage.

"She did, I see. Don't let her get under your skin, Brianna." His tone was light. "She's a staunch Catholic and while she loves me like the son she never had and wouldn't criticize too harshly, she also can't quite set aside her innate horror at the mere idea of sex outside marriage."

Shifting off her legs and lying back down beside her, he stroked a warm hand gently along her flank until she turned her head and looked at him. He was watching her eyes, Brianna realized, gauging her expression as he said;

"However, I'd be lying if I said the thought hadn't occurred to me as the perfect solution to our situation."

"I said I was happy to be a silent partner," Brianna pointed out, and Declan nodded.

"I know, and that's a great solution too, though it does mean we have to put some sort of agreement in place about how much profit gets reinvested and so on. Maybe it's just laziness, but for me at least it would be the best of all possible worlds. Not least because it means you'd stay."

He kissed her shoulder, a slow, tender, open-mouthed kiss, and Brianna just watched him, unsure what to say.

"Can we not get heavy about it right now?" she asked at last. "Can we just… enjoy what this is for a while? Let's talk in a month or so, when we have some idea if we can live and work together without murdering each other on a slightly longer-term basis."

"Wise woman." He kissed her shoulder again before reaching for her lips. "And in the meantime, we can scandalize Molly some more." There was a wicked light in his eyes as he pulled her back into his arms, and Brianna began to laugh.

"I think you've been sex-deprived for too long!"

"You're probably not wrong," he admitted, nuzzling between her breasts and grinding lightly against her thigh, showing her he was aroused again already.

*　　　*　　　*

Declan eased gently back inside Brianna's willing body, groaning with pleasure as she opened to him, curling her long legs around his hips. He hadn't said it, but he knew it wasn't just a few months of abstinence which had his sex drive kicked into such high gear. He'd wanted Brianna from the first time he laid eyes on her, and now he'd got to know and like her as well, his hunger for her was increased tenfold. Marrying her was beginning to sound less farfetched and more appealing by the hour.

As she slept, sated and utterly relaxed, Declan lay wakeful, leaning up on one elbow, watching her peaceful face and wondering what he could do to convince her to stay. Just good sex was no basis for a long-term relationship, and while she clearly enjoyed spending time in the yards and with the horses, he suspected it wouldn't prove fulfilling for her in the long term.

Lying back against the pillows with a sigh, he ordered himself to sleep. The following day would be just as physically demanding as every other on the estate, and he needed to rest.

Right before he drowsed off, his eyes popped open and he began to smile. The thought which had just come to him should give Brianna something to exercise her skills on, for a while at least.

"How much do you know about website design?" he asked when she joined him in the yard the following morning, as he held a mare for the farrier to examine and trim her hooves.

"Quite a bit," Brianna said. "Though it's not my everyday job, I've advised on the redesign of a few websites for clients, and there were several modules on website design and coding in my degree. I wouldn't take on an e-commerce site, though."

"I wouldn't ask you to… but I was thinking of turning you loose on the Leary Estates website. Alec had it put together about ten years ago and all we've really done since is update details on which stallions stand here."

Brianna's eyes sparkled as she met his gaze. "I'd love to! I had a quick look on the website when I first learned about the estate, and was disappointed how bare-bones it is even though the photos are lovely. I could do a lot with it…"

Watching her expression go distant as she began to expound on her ideas, her creative soul clearly revelling in the opportunity, Declan smiled.

"I'll take you up to the office to meet Fionn. She has all the passwords and things. You haven't been in there yet, have you?"

"Only briefly," she said, and he remembered they had indeed looked in when she was pretending to be the business broker's assistant. The office was originally the gate lodge for Galamor, now converted into the place where all their records were kept. A short walk along the drive and they entered the low stone cottage.

Fionn, the office manager, looked up and

nodded to Declan, her fingers dancing over her keyboard as she carried on talking into her telephone headset in Gaelic. Ted was sitting at another desk completing some veterinary paperwork prior to handing it to Mairi, the office junior, to transfer into the computer database and then file. He smiled and greeted Brianna cheerfully.

"And how are you today, lass?"

"Very well, thank you. Declan's asked me to have a look at the website," she said, and Ted nodded enthusiastically.

"That's a raring good idea."

"It certainly is." Fionn ended her call and stood to offer her hand for a handshake, smiling widely. Probably five years older than Brianna, she was plump and cheerful, with a cap of short black curls framing her face. "I've been telling Declan for a while it needs doing, I just don't have the expertise to handle it."

She was obviously delighted to have Brianna joining them, and soon had her set up at a desk with the laptop Brianna had stopped to pick up at the house hooked up to their fast internet connection, and supplied with the necessary passwords to get into the back end of the website. Mairi brought her a cup of coffee with a shy smile, and Brianna settled into her office chair and prepared to get to work.

Spotting Declan lingering by the door, she flipped her hand at him.

"Shoo."

He laughed, and a little to her surprise, came over to bend down and kiss her soundly before turning to head back out again. Blushing bright red, Brianna ducked her head to escape Fionn and Mairi's inquisitive stares, and fortunately neither of them seemed quite confident enough to press her. They returned to their own work and left her in peace to start the website redesign.

CHAPTER SIXTEEN

The days seemed to fly past. Brianna would spend most mornings in the yards with Declan, often riding across to Ballybronn and around the properties with him, before going to the office in the afternoons to work on her own graphic design jobs and the Leary Estates website. She hadn't been confident to put all the changes she'd come up with on line directly, creating a dummy site for Declan to approve first, but he was extremely impressed with what she'd done and told her to put it up immediately. Engagement with the website increased almost immediately, and several previous clients commented on the phone how good it looked.

Brianna honestly couldn't think of a time in her life when she'd felt so happy, so *fulfilled*. Life at Galamor was idyllic, and her relationship with Declan was the icing on the cake. Still, she shied away from thinking about the future, not quite ready to make any commitment just yet.

"Did you pack any nice dresses?" Declan asked unexpectedly one evening. They were relaxing in the huge claw-footed tub in his bathroom, Brianna's head nestled on his shoulder.

"Um... define *nice*," she murmured. "For what occasion?"

"For going to the races." He chuckled and kissed the side of her brow as she turned her head to look at him, blinking. "There's a race meeting in Galway this weekend and we've two horses running."

"Oh." She always forgot the estate had horses who weren't resident there, foals born at the stud to their own mares who went on to race. Kept at training stables around Ireland and England, they were the future bloodstock of the stud. "That sounds really nice."

"We'd be in the owners' pavilion. Folks get pretty dressed up."

Thinking wistfully of her wardrobe at home in Melbourne, Brianna sighed. "I probably don't have anything suitable with me."

"Guess we'd better go down a day early so I can take you shopping then, eh?"

"Take me shopping?" She pinched his arm lightly, laughing. "This is not *Pretty Woman*, Declan. I don't need a makeover and I can buy my own clothes."

"Of course, I just meant you'd want an opportunity to go shopping! And maybe model lots of sexy dresses for me." He poked his tongue out at her, and then took the opportunity to lick her ear, which led to lots of squealing, a tickling match, and half the water in the tub sloshing out onto the floor.

*   *   *

The drive to Galway took about an hour and a half, through some of the most scenic countryside Brianna had ever seen. She spent the whole time gazing out the window, entranced, while Declan drove. She didn't even see his regular glances across at her, his fond smiles.

Declan had booked them a rental cottage just outside the city, where he said he always stayed. A cosy little place, it was set up on a small hill overlooking the water. They stopped by there first to drop off their bags before Declan drove Brianna into town. She wasn't too sure what to expect, wondering if it would be all chain stores on the main street, but was pleasantly surprised to find a couple of independent dress shops, one of them featuring unique creations by a couple of local designers.

She hadn't expected Declan to stay, but to her surprise he sat down in a chair beside the changing room and unfolded the newspaper, smirking at her over the top of it.

"Just waiting for the catwalk show."

"Just for that, I'm not showing you anything!" Brianna was laughing, though, as he gave her sad puppy eyes. "Well. Nothing sexy, anyway," she amended.

"You're not allowed to wear anything sexy to the races. Some smarmy city guy would take one look and steal you away from me."

Was that a hint of vulnerability in his eyes? Pausing in her browsing of the racks, Brianna went over and leaned down to kiss him.

"Impossible," she whispered. "Smarmy city guys have never been my type. If I'd wanted one of those, I met a thousand back in Melbourne. I was waiting for a sexy Irish horse whisperer to sweep me off my feet."

Declan's cheeks flushed a little, but he set his

newspaper down and rose to his feet, catching her around the waist to pull her close. "Say things like that and I'm taking you straight back to the cottage," he said gruffly. "To spend the whole weekend in bed."

"Tempting," she kissed him again before twisting from his light hold. "But you promised me a weekend at the races, and that's what I want. What do you think of that one?"

"Hm?" Declan was still gazing at her, so she crossed the shop to the green dress she'd just spied, took down the hanger to examine it.

"This one. What do you think?"

"That colour would look great on you." He shrugged when she held it up in front of her and raised an interrogative eyebrow. "I know nothing of fashion, Brianna. I have one good suit I wear to the races, and that only because Alec made me buy it."

"Ha, it's easy for men. Nobody even cares if you wear the same suit every day." Taking the dress into the changing room, her voice floated back out to him. "Did you know, there was a presenter on a breakfast TV show in Australia who wore the same suit and tie, with an identical white shirt, on every single show for an entire year, and nobody even noticed? It was an experiment, because he was so shocked by the comments directed at his female co-hosts if they dared to be seen twice in the same outfit."

"I believe it," Declan said. "I've heard women in the owner's enclosures make snide comments if they've seen another woman wearing the same outfit before." He let out a soft whistle as Brianna pushed the curtain back. "Jaysus, you look *amazing*. Trust me, I won't object in the slightest if you want to wear that as many times as you like." He leaned back to take her in, the forest green chiffon clinging in strategic spots, the full skirt swirling to just below her knees.

"I'll need shoes, too."

"Whatever you want," he agreed, in a daze.

"And at least two more dresses."

"Sure."

"And a sports car."

"Of course… wait a minute."

Brianna burst out laughing as he gave her a narrow-eyed look. "Just seeing what I could get you to agree to!" she sang out, darting back inside the change room as he lunged towards her.

"Minx!" he called after her, laughing as well. Truth was, she could buy her own sports car if she wanted one; the estate could certainly afford it. Brianna wasn't accustomed to having money, he thought, not in significant amounts. He knew her father was a successful man, but she'd grown up middle-class with her feet firmly rooted on the ground, not in the least spoiled.

He absolutely adored her, Declan thought, settling back into his chair, though he didn't pick the newspaper up again. Brianna Lane was everything he'd ever wanted, and he'd buy her five damn sports cars if it got her to stay with him instead of getting on the plane back to Australia.

CHAPTER SEVENTEEN

Declan seemed to know absolutely everybody in the horse-racing industry, Brianna thought, and he seemed determined to introduce her to all of them. She was pretty sure most of them assumed she was just his date until he introduced her as "Alastair's niece and heir, and my business partner" at which point, they fell all over themselves to be nice. Well. Some of them did. A couple of the younger women gave her, and the way Declan kept his arm around her, speculative looks and then a rather chilly reception.

It would take her a long time to get everyone's names down, she recognized, but for now Declan gave her a soft running commentary under his breath. This couple owned five active racehorses and three mares now retired to stud; that elderly man, dressed in a threadbare suit older than Brianna, was one of the wealthiest men in Ireland, fingers in every pie.

"And her?" Brianna asked very quietly as a beautiful blonde in a Dolce e Gabbana dress and strappy Jimmy Choo sandals came towards them, preceded by an overpowering waft of sickly perfume.

"Trophy wife," Declan murmured in response, making Brianna choke back a laugh before he stepped forward, all smiles. "Mrs Laoghaire, how lovely to see you!"

"It's Sonya, darling, I've told you a dozen times." She kissed both his cheeks, lingering close to his lips, steely blue eyes giving Brianna a minute examination at the same time.

"How's Fergus?" Declan adroitly avoided agreeing with Sonya, Brianna saw, covering a grin by taking a sip of her champagne.

"Not so well," Sonya pursed her painted pink lips in a pout. "He insisted I come along today, though. Wanted a personal report on Rainmaker's race. I'd love you to come take a look at him, see what you think… this is his last year on the track, of course, and Fergus wouldn't have him stand anywhere else but with you."

"Of course," Declan said amiably. "He's racing in the third, right? We'll come down to the mounting yards. Sonya, you haven't met Brianna yet, have you? Brianna Lane, my co-owner."

Sonya's blue eyes cut back to Declan, widening. "Co-owner?"

"In Leary Estates. Brianna is Alec Leary's great-niece; he named her as joint heir. She's been learning the business."

Brianna smiled and extended her hand; Sonya barely touched it with her fingertips before pulling back, lips pursed.

"I thought it was all yours, Declan."

"That wouldn't have been fair to Alec's blood kin, now would it? Brianna's grandmother was Alec's sister and they were very close, both grew up on Galamor before she married and they emigrated to Australia."

"Australia!" It might have been Jupiter from the expression on Sonya's face. "You're Australian?"

Tempted to play up her accent, Brianna managed to refrain and spoke neutrally. "That's right, but I've never been anywhere as beautiful as Galamor. I can't imagine how my grandmother could bear to leave."

"Hmph." Sonya looked down her nose. "Do you know *anything* about horses?"

"A lot more than I did a few weeks ago." Brianna kept her tone light, though the other woman's tone was starting to irritate her. "I'm looking forward to watching the races today. You have a stallion in the third? Is he the favourite?"

Sonya seemed to thaw a little bit as Brianna made the effort to be open and friendly, though the possessive way she hung onto Declan's arm grated on Brianna's nerves. Declan kept shooting her apologetic looks, though she smiled reassuringly at him, understanding he couldn't ditch Sonya. Reality sucked sometimes, but the fact was the woman and her husband were clients, and wealthy ones at that. Alienating a wealthy couple just because the wife liked to flirt with Declan wasn't good business, and Brianna was mature enough to accept the fact.

Of course, she wasn't exactly overjoyed about it, either. Or the way Sonya kept dropping hints she was all alone at her hotel and Declan should join her for dinner.

"I'm afraid we have plans tonight," Brianna said brightly, deliberately misunderstanding, "but thank you for inviting us!"

Declan's lips twitched, and she knew he was

fighting down a laugh. He had a wicked sense of humour, she'd discovered; they found the same things funny.

Sonya pursed her painted lips again and deliberately turned her back on Brianna, drawing Declan over to the balcony overlooking the track and asking his opinion of the horses entering the mounting yard for the first race.

Laughing quietly to herself, Brianna helped herself to two glasses of champagne from a tray offered by a passing waiter before following them out onto the balcony and slipping a glass into Declan's hand. He shot her a grateful look and took a sip.

Brianna was pretty sure Sonya would have liked to monopolise Declan's attention all afternoon, but they were soon joined by others coming out to watch the first race and Declan took the opportunity to free himself from Sonya's clutches.

"Hey." His warm breath tickled Brianna's ear, and she lowered the binoculars she'd been using to check out the horses and turned to smile at him.

"Hey, yourself."

"Sorry about her."

"You don't need to apologize." Brianna gave him a look of commiseration. "She's very beautiful, but you couldn't have made it more obvious you didn't appreciate her draping herself all over you."

"I respect her husband too much, even if you weren't here with me. Marriage vows are made to be honoured, in my opinion." Slipping an arm around her waist, he glanced down towards the starting line. "Did you put a bet on?"

"Five euros on number eleven."

Pulling his race programme from his pocket, Declan frowned. "Eleven… Fast Lane? Never heard of it."

"Lane. As in, my surname?"

He laughed at her. "You're backing horses based on names?"

"From everything I know about betting on the races, it's as valid a method as any other." She gave him a sardonic look.

"Speak a bit more quietly," he teased, "you'll start a riot in this crowd with those sort of sentiments."

"What would you pick then, with all your superior knowledge?" Brianna folded her arms.

Declan considered the programme. "Number five. Economystery."

"Stupid name. Bet mine beats yours."

"Yeah? A private wager, is it?" Stuffing the programme back into his pocket, he hooked an arm around her waist and pulled her close, breasts against his chest, eyes smouldering down at her. "What will you give me if I win?"

"Nothing you wouldn't be getting anyway," Brianna sassed, making him laugh before he kissed her.

The starter's gun fired as they kissed, and Brianna jumped. Declan laughed huskily against her lips, ending the kiss but keeping her held close.

Everyone else on the balcony must have thought they were mad, Brianna thought after the race, after she cheered number eleven into sixth place and Declan groaned with disgust as his pick ran home a distant last.

Sonya rejoined them then, giving Brianna a condescending smile and putting her hand back on Declan's arm. "Coming down to the mounting yard, darling? By the time we get there through this crush, Rainmaker will be out."

"Of course." Setting his empty glass down, Declan offered his free arm to Brianna. "Bri will be fascinated to see the yards, and I want a word with Sean Murray before the race anyway."

"Sean Murray? The jockey?" Sonya's over-plucked brows drew together. "Why?"

"Because he's riding Ruala Rochelle for us."

Sonya's painted mouth fell open and she drew

back from Declan. "*You* own Ruala Rochelle?"

"Well, the estate does. It's in the programme, didn't you notice?" Declan gave her a saccharine smile, and Brianna had to bite her lips to keep from bursting into laughter. Declan had told her all about Ruala Rochelle on the drive to Galway, a five-year-old mare born from one of Alec's favourites, delivered by Alec and Declan together. From her first year, the filly had shown glimpses of something special, and she hadn't lost a race in over a year. Hot favourite in the afternoon's premium race, she was the runner to beat.

Sonya looked extremely displeased, but she could hardly rescind her invitation now, and since Declan and Brianna obviously intended to go to the mounting yard anyway she obviously figured she might as well accompany them as go alone.

Rainmaker was beautiful, Brianna had to concede, a magnificent black stallion with a crooked white lightning bolt down the centre of his face. He was giving his handler hell in the mounting yard, bucking and rearing, whistling a challenge to another stallion and prancing whenever they got close to a mare. Declan sighed soundlessly and Brianna agreed with him; beautiful the horse might be, but he'd be a pain at the stud.

Ruala Rochelle looked singularly unimpressed

by Rainmaker's antics, walking around quietly on a loose rein, her handler stroking her shoulder and murmuring soft words in her ear. Brianna was surprised by how small the mare seemed. The shortest horse in the mounting yard by quite a margin, she didn't look like a champion.

"You'd be surprised," Declan said with a grin when she muttered the observation to him with a sheepish expression. "Take a look at her from the back. She's got a famously big arse; provides explosive speed in the final sprint other horses can't match. Just watch."

CHAPTER EIGHTEEN

Declan had been quite right about Ruala Rochelle; trailing the field for almost the entire two-mile race, her jockey gave the little mare her head with a quarter mile to go and she showed a turn of explosive speed which had to be seen to be believed. Rainmaker looked positively indignant as he chased Ruala Rochelle's famously large arse across the finish line.

Brianna finally understood why Declan had been so insistent she'd need a nice outfit, as he escorted her to the winner's circle and insisted she accept the large silver plate. Cameras flashed, making her blink, though she did her best to keep her smile fixed in place as she patted Ruala

Rochelle's sweating neck, and afterwards a couple of reporters came up and asked Declan to introduce her.

"And will you be staying in Ireland, Miss Lane?" one of them asked, holding his phone towards her like a microphone, obviously recording her words.

"To be honest I can't think of any reason to go back to Australia," she said with a laugh, and felt Declan's arm tighten around her waist. She turned her head to smile at him, seeing the blaze of emotion in his eyes.

He couldn't get her away from the reporters and to a quiet spot fast enough. They ended up somewhere under the grandstand while the crowd cheered on the runners in the next race.

"Say you meant it. Say you'll stay," he demanded, his brogue thickening with emotion so she could barely understand him.

"I'm staying."

He kissed her then, fierce and passionate, kissing off all her lipstick as he ravished her mouth. Not that Brianna cared. She didn't care when he took her hand and led her out to where they'd parked the car, either, driving them straight back to their holiday cottage to spend the rest of the day in bed. After all, their other horse wasn't running until the following day.

*   *   *

Arriving back at Galamor two days later, they stumbled into the house laughing joyously, hands all over each other. Brianna teased Declan about running straight down to the yards and checking on the horses; he pinched her bottom.

"Don't think so, missy. Up those stairs with you… oh."

There were two people standing halfway up the stairs, mouths agape as Brianna rushed forward, giggling. Her foot hit the bottom step and she saw them too.

"Mum? Dad!"

Behind her, Declan said several things in Gaelic she was pretty sure were curses before moving up alongside her.

"Mr and Mrs Lane, what a lovely surprise. I'm Declan O'Siorain. Welcome to Galamor."

"What are you *doing* here?" Brianna gaped as her parents moved on down to the bottom of the steps to embrace her. "When did you arrive?"

"This morning." Her father was giving Declan a very narrow-eyed look as he answered her second question first. "And your mother has been after me to fly over ever since the business valuation came back at almost four times Mr O'Siorain's offer. She thought you might need my advice, and legal expertise, to handle the sale."

Declan sucked in his breath, and Brianna shook her head quickly at him before turning back to her parents. "Come on into the lounge and I'll make some coffee," she suggested. "You must be exhausted; it took me weeks to get over the jet lag after I arrived!"

"I'll head down to the yards and catch up with what's been going on," Declan said hastily.

Good plan, Brianna thought. Getting him temporarily out of sight was probably a good plan, especially considering the glare her father was still directing his way.

"I hope it's all right," Molly said anxiously when Brianna hurried into the kitchen, "but your parents turned up on the doorstep right in the middle of breakfast, I wasn't sure what to do, and I knew you'd be back this morning…"

"It's fine, Molly." Brianna gave the housekeeper a hug and a kiss. "Could I beg you for a pot of coffee in the lounge?"

"Of course, I'll bring it in shortly. Did you enjoy the races, then?"

"We had a wonderful weekend," Brianna said

brightly, neglecting to mention they'd barely spent any time at the racetrack, electing instead to spend most of the weekend in bed. Fortunately Molly took her words at face value and nodded as Brianna made a hasty exit.

Pausing outside the lounge, Brianna took a deep breath. While she'd talked to her parents at least once a week via Skype, she'd been deliberately vague about her plans, just telling them she was enjoying learning about the business and about the man her great-uncle had been. She'd avoided talking about Declan at all, thinking she'd be able to ease slowly into explaining how she'd fallen in love with him.

"Brianna, I know you're standing outside the door," her father's voice said dryly, and she winced. "I heard your footsteps. Come on in here and tell us what's going on, because it's clear you've been somewhat less than forthcoming with us."

Caught out, she winced and pushed the door open slowly. Her mother was sitting on the couch by the window, her father standing looking out at the view over the lake. He turned to face her as she entered and shook his head.

"We didn't raise you to lie to us, Bri." Sally Lane was the one who spoke, though, her voice reproachful.

Brianna's temper flared, but she took another deep breath and kept a lid on it. "I didn't lie to you. I may not have been entirely forthcoming, but that was because I wasn't sure myself how I felt and what decisions I was going to make."

"What decision is there to be made?" Sally threw up her hands. "O'Siorain made you a lowball offer, and once the valuation came back he obviously coerced you into sleeping with him so you'll accept it and let him have your inheritance at a fraction of what it's worth!"

"For the record, I was sleeping with him before the complete valuation came back," Brianna fired back, and saw her mother blanch.

"Brianna!" Sally gasped, hand to her heart.

"Oh, come on. This is the twenty-first century. Don't be prudish."

"Brianna, please don't speak to your mother like that," her father said, his tone mild, but then he rarely raised his voice.

"What exactly would you like me to say, Dad? It's quite clear you've come over here because you don't trust my judgement." Annoyed beyond measure, Brianna folded her arms across her chest and stared him down.

"Well, we were right not to, apparently!" Sally flared. "Since you're sleeping with Declan…"

"Do you seriously think, just because of that, I'm going to meekly hand over everything to him? Don't insult me!" Brianna was steaming. "I'm happier here at Galamor than I've ever been. I feel like I've come home, and I fully intend to stay, whether or not Declan and I eventually split or not."

Sally looked upset, but Andrew considered Brianna silently, nodding.

"You look well," he said unexpectedly. "You've got colour in your cheeks, and your eyes are shining. Don't you think, Sally?"

"I suppose," Sally said grudgingly. "The fresh air must be good for you. It's certainly beautiful here." She glanced out at the view over the lake.

"It really is," Brianna said enthusiastically, sensing her parents weakening. "Come for a walk and let me show you around the place."

She half-expected them to decline, but they both agreed, and five minutes later she was showing them proudly around the main yard.

"Impressive," Andrew murmured, sharp eyes taking in the huge complex, the stable hands industriously cleaning out stables while their occupants spent time out in the fields.

They found Declan with Ted the vet, examining a mare who wouldn't put her front hoof on the ground.

"Abscess?" Brianna asked, leaning over the stable door.

"Reckon so," Ted said gloomily. "She's been lame for a few days, but I hoped it was only a hoof bruise. Got to take an X-ray to be sure, but I'm thinking I'll have to drain and pack it. Oh, hello," he said as he saw Brianna's parents. "Didn't know we were expecting visitors?" Ted looked inquiringly at Duncan.

"My parents," Brianna said.

Ted's expression was a sight to behold as Brianna made the introductions. He begged off from shaking hands, citing possible cross-contamination, but said how pleased he was to meet them.

"Brianna's been great to have around," he declared. "Already reworked the website from the ground up, you should see the wonderful new photos she took and put up there. Our enquiries have soared, haven't they, Declan?"

"That they have," Declan agreed. "In fact, we're increasing fees for three of our stallions effective immediately, based on the surge in enquiries." Leaning on the stable door, he offered up his best smile, and Brianna actually saw the moment her mother melted.

Brianna hid a smile behind her hand as they

were walking back to the house and Sally said "Declan's very charming, darling."

"Actually I'm not sure *charming* is the right word," Brianna said thoughtfully. "It implies a certain degree of artfulness, and that's not Declan at all. He's a genuinely honest, thoughtful, *nice* man."

"I see." Sally glanced at her sideways. "You're in love with him, then?"

"I am." While she hadn't said it aloud to Declan yet, there had been no doubt in Brianna's mind for quite some time now. "He's wonderful, Mum. When you get to know him, you'll understand. He has no intention of cheating me... when we realised how high the valuation was, he was utterly distraught, trying to figure out a way to get me my fair share without having to sell off any of the property. This place is everything to him, and it's quickly becoming everything to me."

"You don't see yourself coming home, then?" her father asked a little sadly.

"To what, Dad? To go back and sit behind a desk all day again, when I know I can have this - that I have a *right* to this?" Brianna turned and gestured, encompassing all they saw with a sweep of her arm. "I never knew Great-Uncle Alec, but everyone here did, and they all tell me the same thing. That he loved this place more than life itself."

"And he left you half of it," her father said with a slow nod.

"Let's be honest, he could have left everything to Declan, who was like a son to him, and we'd never even have known." Brianna looked out at the lake, breathing in the fresh country air, the scents which had become so familiar to her. "Yet, he took the time to find me, have me investigated, and leave me half of all this. Selling it would be an insult to his memory."

"I wish I'd known him," Sally said wistfully.

"Me too. I've learned a lot about him, from Declan, Ted, Molly, and all the others here who'd known him for years, and about Grandmother Sinead too. There's a beautiful portrait of her as a young girl upstairs, actually. Would you like to see it?"

Sally accepted with delight, and Brianna smiled to herself as she mounted the stairs arm in arm with her mother. It would take a little time, and probably lot more exposure to Declan's good nature, but they'd come to understand her choice, she was sure.

CHAPTER NINETEEN

Both Sally and Andrew had softened considerably by dinnertime, when they sat down with Brianna and Declan in the formal dining-room to one of Molly's fabulous dinners. Brianna had debated eating in the kitchen with the live-in hands, but Molly wouldn't hear of it.

"We're putting our best foot forward for your parents and no mistake," she told Brianna severely.

"Yes, Molly," Brianna said laughingly. "Should I start polishing the best silver?"

"It's kept very well polished, thank you," Molly put her hands on her hips and shook her head. "Get on with you now."

Her parents were having an afternoon nap to get past the worst of the jet lag, Wondering whether she should go up to the office, Brianna nevertheless decided against it. She didn't want to come back to find her father and Declan in some sort of standoff. She headed up to Declan's room to unpack instead – she'd never even slept in the room which was supposedly 'hers'.

"Hey, gorgeous," Declan's drawl made her jump and spin around, clutching at her heart. He stood leaning against the doorframe, grinning at her. "You sure you're allowed to be in here?"

"Oh, shush." She hurried over to grab his arm and pull him into the room, closing the door as quietly as she could. "Keep your voice down!"

"Can I just point out this is *our* house?" Declan was obviously laughing at her. Pulling her close, he nuzzled at her neck. "You're adorable when you're being coy," he murmured.

Sighing, Brianna melted into his embrace. "I'm sorry. It's difficult. I know they love me and they really do have my best interests at heart, but…"

"But suddenly you feel as though you're fourteen again?" Declan guessed, and she laughed self-deprecatingly.

"I'm afraid so. Their coming here unannounced basically shows how little faith they have in my judgement, doesn't it?"

"I think it shows how much they care about you, *a chuisle*." He stroked her hair, holding her against him. "Don't knock having parents who love you, Bri. I'd give a great deal to have my mother here again, or Alec."

"Oh!" Startled, she looked up at him. "I didn't think. I'm sorry."

"It's fine." Gently, he brushed his mouth over hers. "We'll humour them until they understand, *a chuisle*."

"You said that before… *acushla*. What does it mean?"

"My pulse." Taking her hand in his, he brought it to his chest, over his heart. "It beats for you, Brianna. It has since the day you walked in here and helped me with the Lass foaling, even knowing I was in the mood to strangle you."

"Oh, Declan." Gazing up into his eyes, she knew the time was right to say the words. "I love you."

"I love you too, *a chuisle*, but surely you knew that already?"

"I hoped." She watched, wide-eyed, as Declan took a step back and sank to one knee.

"Don't think having your parents here forced my hand," he said, dipping one hand into his pocket, "because I bought this in Galway while you were shoe shopping and fully intended to ask you this week anyway. Will you marry me, Brianna Lane?"

The ring he held up was perfect in its understated simplicity; a full circle of diamonds set deeply into a gold channel, there were no raised stones to snag or catch. It was perfect for someone who handled horses every day.

"Oh." Brianna's throat was so full she couldn't get a word out, her eyes overflowing with happy tears. Nodding frantically, she held her hand out and Declan slid the ring onto her finger, his own grin threatening to split his face in two.

"The only problem," Brianna said quite a few minutes and quite a lot of kisses later, "is that my parents are going to want us to get married in Melbourne."

"Well, as to that," Declan said, "I might have had some thoughts in that direction. Ruala Rochelle's entered to run in the Melbourne Cup, you see, and I was thinking we might fly over there to watch and get married there so your parents can be there… and then we can come home and have a second round here. All the estate folks will want to come, and we could turn it into a big celebration, invite all the horsey folk I know."

"That might be the biggest wedding Ireland's ever seen, then," Brianna teased with a happy laugh, but the truth was she didn't care in the least where they got married or who attended. All that mattered was Declan was the groom.

"You'll be the most beautiful bride Ireland's ever seen," Declan said thickly, his voice deepening to a husky rasp as he lifted her hand and kissed the ring on her finger.

Smiling at him lovingly, Brianna reached up to hook her arms around his neck. "I daresay Mum and Dad will sleep another hour or so," she said coquettishly, "and we really should celebrate our engagement."

He didn't need any further invitation, carrying her to the bed and stripping both of them to bare skin in double-quick time, laving kisses over Brianna's naked body until she was moaning and begging him to hurry up.

"No rush, *a chuisle*," he said hoarsely, positioning himself over her. "We've got the rest of our lives, after all."

Brianna sobbed with pleasure as Declan eased slowly inside her, bending his head to catch one plump, rosy nipple between his lips and suckle on it. His hips rolled gently, creating an unbearable tension inside her until she dug her heels into his ass with frustration.

"More!" she shouted, forgetting entirely they weren't alone in the house until Declan snorted with laughter and kissed her quickly to quiet her. The moment was almost lost as they both succumbed to the giggles.

"D'you think they heard?" Brianna whispered breathlessly.

"I doubt it. Galamor's got thick walls," Declan got out through his laughter. "But even if they did... it's our house, remember?" Easing out of her, he tugged on her hip, encouraging her to roll over. "Here. Bury your face in the pillow. You can yell as much as you like then."

She knew she'd want to yell quite a lot when he took her from behind, because it always felt so damn good. Bunching the pillow in her hands, she bit down as he slid back into her, suppressing her ecstatic moan.

"Now I've just got to worry about my own noises," Declan said hoarsely, strong hands settling on her hips, "because damn, Bri..."

She thrust back at him demandingly and he said several Gaelic curse words before giving her what she wanted, hips snapping back and forth to shuttle his cock roughly in and out of her sopping channel.

Even muffled by a pillow, Brianna was sure her

shrieks of pleasure were pretty loud, especially combined with Declan's groans. She just hoped Galamor's walls were as soundproof as Declan seemed to think.

*　　　*　　　*

Sally seemed considerably softened at dinner, especially once she'd tasted Molly's delicious baked trout, and though Andrew was a little more reserved Brianna saw his quiet smiles and knew he was accepting of the situation. He was just worried about her future security, and she couldn't blame him for that, especially considering his profession.

"Though perhaps I should take you aside to speak to you, Andrew," Declan said towards the end of the meal, "I'm not a great believer in leaving women out of decisions, let alone important ones. I've already asked Brianna and she accepted me, so all I have left to do is ask you and Sally if you'll give us your blessings."

"For what?" Andrew said, and Brianna smiled to herself as she saw his lips quirk up with amusement.

For all he'd sounded confident, Declan wasn't in the least, and he grew suddenly flustered as he realised he hadn't been specific enough. "Oh. Uh, uh, Jaysus, I'm making a muck of this. Words aren't my strong point," he confessed.

"Oh, I don't know," Sally said. She'd had a couple of glasses of wine and become almost giggly. "The accent's so divine I don't care much what you're saying."

Both Brianna and her father had to stifle their laughter with napkins, and Declan chuckled, the tension of the moment broken.

"I take it you won't mind becoming my mother-in-law, then, Sally?" he teased gently.

"Mother-in-law? You mean – you asked – you're getting *married*?" The last word was a shocked squeal, and for a moment Brianna was afraid Sally was going to make a scene, but she needn't have been concerned. A moment later Sally was up on her feet and practically throwing herself on Declan, hugging him tight. "Oh, that's so wonderful! Come here, darling girl!"

The hug bestowed on Brianna was the tightest she could ever remember receiving from her mother. Her father smiled benignly at them both, waiting until Sally finally calmed down before standing up and reaching to shake Declan's hand.

"While I don't know you well yet," he said, "I do have faith in my daughter's judgement, and if she says you're a man worthy of her, that's plenty good enough for me. Welcome to the family... son."

Declan looked surprised before gulping visibly and turning to look at Brianna. She gave him a warm, loving smile, understanding just what being called *son* might mean to a man who had never known a father.

"Where are you going to get married?" Sally asked excitedly. "And when? And, oh my God, what am I going to *wear*?"

EPILOGUE

They ended up getting married in Ireland in late September, the local priest presiding over the ceremony in a packed-out church, before flying out to Australia a week later. Ruala Rochelle was already there with her entourage, racing in a couple of warm-up races before her big day at the Melbourne Cup, the 'race that stops a nation' as the Australians call it.

The newspapers picked up on the story of an Australian girl inheriting a half-share in an Irish racing stud and then marrying her co-heir, and as co-owners of a Melbourne Cup hopeful they appeared in quite a few articles and magazines, delighting Brianna's mother.

"You look beautiful, darling," Sally wiped away a tear as she gazed at Brianna, once again wearing her wedding dress, this time for a smaller ceremony held in her parents' back garden.

Andrew had no words, but he held out his arm for his daughter and pressed a kiss to the side of her brow. She'd allowed him to draft an iron-clad prenuptial agreement protecting her half of the inheritance no matter what, and both she and Declan had happily signed it, secure in the knowledge the enforcement of its provisions would never be necessary.

Brianna smiled to herself as her father escorted her outside. They were waiting until after the Cup, run the following Tuesday, to share their other news; the fact that the Leary Estates would have a new heir in about seven months. She and Declan were already agreed on names; if they had a son, they would name him Alec, and a daughter would be Sinead.

How could she ever have imagined, six months ago, she'd be here today, marrying the man of her dreams? And it was all thanks to an entirely unexpected inheritance, from the great-uncle she'd never even known, but who had chosen her as his heir instead of her mother, maybe guessing that she'd be more curious and wouldn't sell sight unseen. Had he perhaps thought she and Declan might make a match of it? She smiled at the thought.

"Thanks, Uncle Alec," she whispered to the heavens as she proceeded towards Declan on her father's arm. "Thanks for everything."

~ The End ~

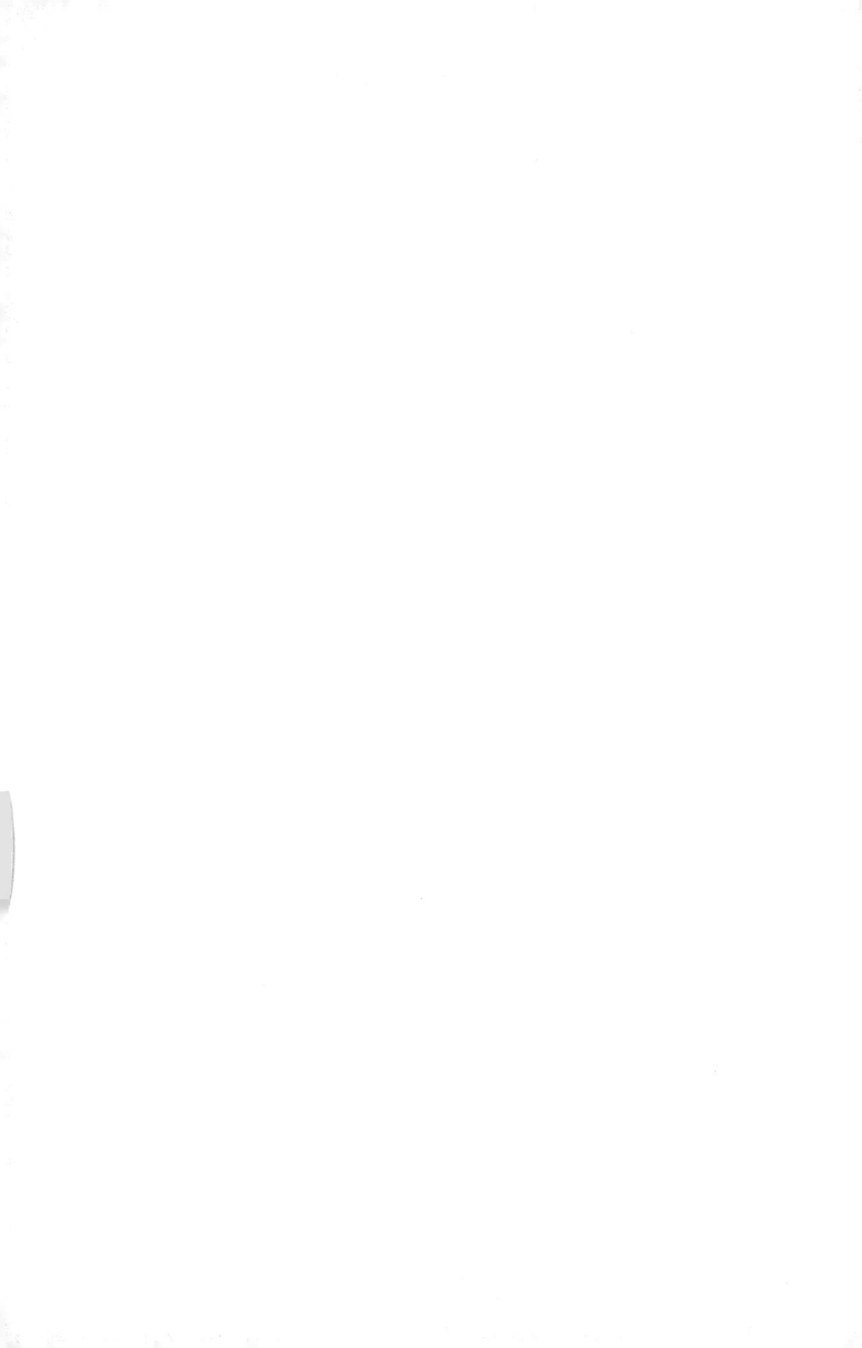

ABOUT THE AUTHOR

Born in North Wales, Caitlyn lived and travelled all over the UK and Europe before falling in love with the man of her dreams and emigrating to Australia.

Today, she lives in sunny Queensland with her husband and two sons. Her romances feature the kind of people you might actually meet in real life, falling in love and finding their happily ever afters.

Learn more about Caitlyn and her books, and join her mailing list, at caitlynlynch.com